GIRL 38

Ewa Jozefkowicz grew up in Ealing, and studied English Literature at UCL. Her debut novel *The Mystery of the Colour Thief* was published by Zephyr in 2018. She currently works in marketing, and lives in Highbury, north London, with her husband and twin girls.

Also by Ewa Jozefkowicz

The Mystery of the Colour Thief

GIRL 38

FINDING A FRIEND

EWA JOZEFKOWICZ

ZEPHYR

First published in the UK by Zephyr,
an imprint of Head of Zeus, in 2019

9 7 5 3 1 2 4 6 8

A catalogue record for this book is available
from the British Library.

ISBN (HB): 9781786698971
ISBN (E): 9781786698964

Illustrations © Anna Hymas
Train illustration © Luna Aït-Oumeghar

Printed and bound in Great Britain
by CPI Group (UK) Ltd, Croydon CR0 4YY

Head of Zeus Ltd
First Floor East
5–8 Hardwick Street
London EC1R 4RG

WWW.HEADOFZEUS.COM

For my grandmother

ONE

*C*aptain Eagle Heart had done all he could, *but everyone on board could hear the engine struggling. An ear-splitting screech ripped the air. Some of the crew started to scream, waiting for the crash, but Girl 38 knew that they were going to make it. She wasn't like the other girls. She was a highly-skilled space-traveller – cool-headed, noble and brave—*

'Kat, what are you doing? Drawing that stupid comic again? Look…' Gem hissed at me. 'He's here. Apparently he has some news for us. I overheard him talking to Miss Seymour in the corridor.'

I added the finishing touches to crazy, fiery sparks exploding from the spacecraft before I looked up and saw Mr Kim strolling into the classroom. I immediately felt my face heat up. I'd forgotten how tall he was – he looked like one of those celebrity basketball players. He'd had a haircut over the holidays and got different glasses.

I glanced at my sketch of Captain Eagle Heart and regretted getting so far ahead with it. He was modelled on Mr Kim, and I could now see that his new look suited the character much better. But then again, maybe it was for the best. Gem would have definitely noticed the similarity and I wouldn't have heard the end of it.

'Greetings, all,' he said to us, giving an exaggerated wave. I heard Gem sigh. Unlike me, she didn't think much of him, but then sometimes I wondered whether she thought much of anyone apart from Arun.

'Welcome to a new term. I hope you all had a great six weeks off. I'm sure you have some wonderful stories to tell. Save them until lunchtime if you possibly can though, because I need to take the register and then I have an important announcement.'

I could tell that Gem was distracted – something, or rather someone, across the room had caught her eye. She whispered from behind her long, dark hair, 'I'm going to go on a date with him this term.'

For a second I thought she meant Mr Kim and I wondered if she'd lost the plot, but she was gazing at Arun, who was busy looking at his phone under the desk.

'What? Seriously?' I asked her.

'Yeah, my horoscope said so. It'll probably happen in September, maybe October at the latest.'

'Right.' I didn't know what else to say.

'Gemma, I'm sure you're not listening,' Mr Kim said. 'And if you *were* listening, you might find that you're interested. As I was saying, Julius will be joining us tomorrow. His family are still in the process of moving, so unfortunately he couldn't make it in today. But I want you all to make him feel welcome when he starts. He's a top swimmer and he comes from a fascinating part of the country, so he'll have loads to tell you. Now... next on my list – your timetables.'

A red spot appeared high up on Gem's cheek.

She'd always had that spot. The first time I'd noticed it was when we were in nursery and there was a prize for the most helpful person in our class. It went to a girl called Molly. Gem didn't cry or anything – I just saw the red spot appear and then her fists clenched tightly at her sides. My own stomach knotted with nerves when I saw it. I guessed that, right now, she was already prickling at the thought of Julius maybe being better than her at swimming, perhaps other things too. It was unlikely, of course, as Gem's the swimming champion, and best in our class at most things. Even so, she doesn't like anyone or anything that might be a threat.

I've known Gem since we were three, which is a super long time – over nine years. We met at the gates of nursery on our first day there. She was shorter than me and wore a big fluffy white dress that made her look a bit like a snowman.

'Want to be my friend?' she'd asked.

I'd nodded. It was as simple as that. I thought I was lucky, because there were always a lot of people who wanted to be Gem's friend, but she only chose me. And she looked out for me after that. If you weren't Gem's friend then you fell into a category of people who she could, at any moment, decide were her enemies. It wasn't good to get on the wrong side of her.

Throughout primary school it had always been the two of us. We sat next to each other in all our lessons, we were always partners in any activities and we were round at each other's houses most nights.

Dad seemed to think that I could do with mixing in a bigger crowd, but I told him that I didn't need to. I had Gem.

Then, at the end of Year Six, there was a panic, as Mum and Dad wanted me to go to the Castle School, which is a private girls' school in town. Two sisters, Maisie and Abigail, on my street go there. They wear uniforms with long, pleated skirts and they sound posh. I wouldn't go, of course, unless Gem did, and it turned out that her mum would never have been able to afford it – not with four other children. It wouldn't have been fair if she'd only sent Gem.

'I don't care!' Gem shouted at me when she found out that her mum wouldn't even agree to them going to look round on an open day. 'I don't want to go there anyway. You sit in your lah-di-dah castle while the rest of us carry on here in the real world. I knew you were stuck up! It's always about you and nobody else.'

None of that was true, especially not the last part. In fact, I was always thinking about Gem. I cried and cried. I was scared of losing her. I begged my parents not to send me to 'the stupid castle'. I got myself into such a state that I made myself ill. In the end, unbelievably, they gave in and I went to Marley High with Gem and most of the others from our primary school class.

Of course, I thought that it would be the same as ever – me and her – but, no. Gem decided that she needed a bigger gang. First, she made friends with Ruby, a tall, thin girl with pale brown skin and her hair done in hundreds of little plaits. Then Ruby introduced her to Dilly, who was round-faced and ginger, and super enthusiastic about everything. So our two became a four and things weren't the same after that.

I still sit next to Gem but we don't do anything just the two of us anymore. Ruby and Dilly are always there. It's not that I don't like them, but it seems like most of the things they do are to impress Gem or to make her laugh. Guess I do that too. If they don't succeed, they're miserable for the rest of the day.

Today, Gem gathered the three of us round her at lunch and asked casually, 'This Julius. What d'you reckon?'

'Sounds like a Vilk to me.'

Ruby and Dil looked confused, but Gem knew what I meant. It was our private joke; the Vilks were the enemy in *Girl 38*, which I'd only shown to her. But she didn't laugh like I thought she would.

'He might be all right,' Gem said, pretending for a second to be cool about it. 'Who knows? Maybe he'll create a bit of excitement. Our class is so *boring* these days.'

When she said that, I wondered for a moment if she meant me, and I felt a tingling of nerves in my stomach. I had a strange intuition that this new guy was about to change everything.

TWO

Weirdly, I found myself thinking about Julius on the way home. In my head, he was tall, muscular and menacing – like the King of the Vilks – a force to be reckoned with. Just as weirdly, part of me secretly hoped that he might challenge Gem. Nobody in our class had dared so far. I know she was my best friend, but she could be so bossy sometimes.

'Good afternoon! You would prefer vegetable casserole or burger and chips tonight?' Lena called from the kitchen as she heard me come in. It made me laugh, the way she always sounded so formal. She popped up suddenly in the hall, her hair wet and her cheeks flushed. She was still cradling her phone between her shoulder and her ear. 'Shhh…' she whispered into it. 'One minute, baby.'

I wasn't sure why she felt the need to be so secretive. I'd found out about her boyfriend a couple of days after she arrived with us. I soon realised that he probably came to the house when I was at school and Mum and Dad were at work. The first time I worked out he existed was when I saw a pair of trainers, definitely not Dad's, in the hall, and then a week or so later, I saw him in the garden, smoking. I wondered if they'd met at language school.

I'm not certain that Lena always remembered my name, and her cooking was pretty terrible most of the time, but she was definitely more interesting than the other au pairs we'd had.

'Burger, please,' I said. I doubted that she'd ever intended to make the casserole, but she felt she needed to pretend there was a healthy option.

'Allow me twenty minutes,' she said, brushing down her apron furiously. It was covered in Chester's hair – Lena's relationship with Chester was a love-hate one. He adored her (mainly because she fed him), and she absolutely hated him (mainly because he shed his long ginger cat hair all over her designer skinny jeans and everywhere else).

Chester was sunning himself at the end of our garden and I walked out to join him. I suppose it's one of the good things about Mum and Dad working such long hours – we can afford a huge house and lots of outdoor space. I even have my own private little corner of the garden to sit in. I like to work on *Girl 38* there.

I sat down in my usual spot and took out the exercise book. Chester stretched next to me, and then parked himself on my lap as I worked.

Girl 38 stepped out of the remains of the Infiniship, along with First Mate Hawk Eye, the second in command. The first mate was tall and frightening, with beautiful jet-black hair and a sharp fringe. She had carefully selected Girl 38 to accompany her on the first mission on the new planet, which they had named U for utopia. They were hopeful it would form a happy home for them, but they needed to check the terrain. Girl 38 was fearless. She knew the part she had to play.

Luckily, everyone had survived the crash with only minor injuries, though the ship was in tatters. The crew were working hard to fix it, but in the meantime, they had to begin their search for food, as their supplies were running low. Hawk Eye knew about the dangers that lay ahead and was planning to use Girl 38 as a shield in case they came across any predators, especially the Vilks, who were humans with wolf-heads. They had bright yellow eyes and long snouts with huge fangs.

I was beginning to draw the outline of a Vilk when I heard a wail. It came from behind me, from the space between the bushes where the fence had fallen down. I turned in my seat and saw what looked like a blue, furry mound wobbling in the densest corner of the Jankowski Jungle.

A sliver of fear wormed its way down the back of my neck. I barely admitted it to myself, but I'd always been a bit wary of our next-door neighbour, Mrs Jankowski, mainly because she was such a mystery. I knew that she'd lived at number thirty-four for years before we moved in last summer. Dad said that she'd been very friendly when he'd spoken to her, but I'd always been too busy to take any notice of her. And Gem said there were lots of signs that pointed to her being entirely mad. 'Just look at the place,' she said. 'It's overgrown and creepy. Who knows what it's like inside, or what goes on in there?'

It was true. Both of Mrs Jankowski's gardens, front and back, were massively overgrown. The back one was so bad, I called it 'the jungle'. Rose bushes had rambled out of control. Their thin, thorny branches scraped the air like gnarled fingers. The grass hadn't been mown in years, so in parts it was knee-high. The whole place was covered with dandelion-clocks that had multiplied in their hundreds; their fluffy seed-heads scattered like tiny white parachutes in the wind. In the front, closest to the fence, there was a bed of nettles so thick that if somebody accidentally fell into them, they would have been covered in nettle rash from head to toe.

The undergrowth was overshadowed by a couple of oak trees that nobody had ever bothered to cut back. A red bird house was fixed to the branches of one, which I'd only noticed because of the pigeons and sparrows that would regularly descend on it. They made so much noise over their supper that Chester would bristle with annoyance as he sat in his favourite patch on the window sill.

'Is anyone there?' I asked.

When I heard a reply, I went into *Girl-38* mode, jumped over the broken fence before I'd had time to think about what I was doing and was next to her in seconds. I yanked what I soon realised was a navy fleece blanket from her head and pulled her into a sitting position.

'Mrs Jankowski, are you OK?'

She was shaking, sitting there on the ground, and I was worried that she was hurt. But then I heard a giggle and saw that she was shaking with laughter, and without knowing why, I started laughing too.

I helped her to her feet and she looked at me, the corners of her eyes scrunched up. She had so many wrinkles, and tiny, bird-like hands. Her hair wasn't short like most old ladies', but long, thick and grey. She'd pinned it in an elaborate twist. When she stood, unsteadily, I realised that she wasn't wearing old-lady clothes either, but a white shirt, tucked into a dark blue skirt with beautiful peacocks on it. Their feathers were woven from coloured thread that shimmered in the sunlight.

'I am a fool. I know I should not wear this ridiculous skirt. It is much too long for me anyway. Sometimes, in my head, I am still a young, tall beauty, when in reality I am a shrunken, shrivelled old raisin.'

I'd never noticed her accent before, but then again, we'd never said much more than 'hello' to each other. Now I could hear that her words were soft and slightly whispery, and her 'a's and 'o's a bit longer than mine.

'You're not a shrivelled raisin,' I said to her. I don't normally speak to people I don't know very well, but there was something about Mrs Jankowski that suddenly made me feel as though I was talking to a friend.

'Ha, well, if not a shrivelled raisin, then definitely a silly witch, as they say in my country. Do you know, I was thinking that I could have a little picnic out here? I saw the sunshine through the window, and suddenly I wanted nothing more than to be outside. I think to myself: *Ania, why not take out this blanket, bring your food and spend the evening sunbathing?* I forgot that, with all the weeds, there wouldn't be a flat patch anywhere – and that even if I managed to sit, I would not be able to get back up. And do you know the worst part? I managed to trip myself before I even reached my destination.'

'I can help you if you want?' What made me say that? *Girl 38* again? I wondered what Gem would think about me talking to the witch next door. Except it turned out that she wasn't a witch at all.

'You've already helped me,' she said, smiling. 'And I am grateful, my dear.'

'No, I mean – I could weed your garden for you. We have a great lawnmower, so I could mow the grass.'

'You are very kind, but I am sure that you have many more exciting ways to be spending your evenings.'

'I'd like to.'

I picked up the rug and folded it, then offered her my arm to lead her back inside. She felt so light that I was certain a strong gust of wind would blow her away at any moment. I wondered how she managed to get around.

'Can I make you a cup of tea to say thank you? Do you drink tea?' she asked. 'In Poland, we drink it with lemon and a little spoon of honey, or sugar. Or I can see if I have some lemonade for you in the fridge? I don't know what young people drink these days.'

'I'd love a Polish tea,' I said. I don't know why, but she seemed so frail. I could sense that she wanted me to stay.

We were in her conservatory which faced the back garden, a beautiful room, compared to the jungle. There were two elegant armchairs, printed in swirly patterns. Between them, a tiny coffee table stood, its top painted in a chessboard pattern. She motioned for me to sit down. I noticed that there wasn't a TV in sight. Instead, in the corner of the room, I spotted an easel covered with a sheet.

She brought the tea in mismatched mugs – one was chipped and had a pattern of red frogs on it, and the other was shaped a bit like a tiny vase and had a fancy gold handle. I loved that she handed me this one and took the frogs for herself. Her hands shook ever so slightly and I could see the concentration on her face as she placed the mugs on the table.

'Have you been painting?' I asked.

'Oh, no. Well, I was many years ago. Not recently.' She waved the idea away, as if it wasn't even worth talking about.

'Could I see?' I love art and although I'm only good at comics myself, I enjoy looking at paintings – from stormy landscapes to close-up portraits of strangers I'll never meet. I've always thought that you could find out so much about an artist from what they painted.

Mrs Jankowski hesitated. Then she cocked her head, to indicate that I could take off the sheet.

I leaped up quickly before she changed her mind and pulled it off to reveal a beautiful pencil sketch of a girl. She looked as though she might be my age, maybe slightly older. She had a thick plait, snaking its way round her neck, and long eyelashes that flicked out at the edges. She seemed to be looking straight at me, but in a friendly way. Her eyes had been coloured a brilliant blue, but the rest of the portrait was unfinished, as if the artist had abandoned it halfway through.

'It's awesome, Mrs Jankowski,' I told her honestly. 'Is it somebody you know?'

'Call me Ania. I am old, but not *that* old,' she said. 'And this is Mila. She's a friend from when I was thirteen years old. We had a lot of adventures together.' She was still smiling, but I could see that her smile didn't quite stretch all the way to her eyes. She covered up the portrait again with the sheet, as if she didn't want to look at it for too long.

'Really? What kind of adventures?' I wondered whether Mila ever made her do the sort of stuff that Gem made me do.

'Oh, she once sent me on a search for her across the whole country.' She lowered her voice and whispered, 'I jumped from a moving train, trying to find her.'

I looked at her to see whether she was joking, but she seemed serious.

'You jumped from a train? What sort of train?' I was imagining the types of trains that I'd taken to see Uncle Pete down in Devon, but she must have meant something entirely different. You couldn't jump from a moving train – that would be madness.

'It is a long story, Katherine – a long and winding story. I think you do not have time to hear it,' she said. 'I am sure you were doing something important before I disturbed you with my fall.'

'I was drawing,' I said. I was amazed that she'd remembered my name from when Dad had introduced us all, months ago.

'Will you show me?' she asked.

'Oh, it's nothing – just me doodling. It's not exactly art.' Even so, I felt compelled to go back to my garden and return with my exercise book.

Even Gem hadn't seen this much. I'd sort of given up showing her these days. Ania was the first person that I'd ever shown the whole thing. It was as if I knew that she would understand it.

'You have a talent,' she said. 'Girl 38? I can see that she is bold and she tries to overcome her fears. I suppose you turn bold if there is something that you feel strongly about. I would be very interested to read more when you finish it. That is, if you allow me, of course.'

I thought for a moment. 'I'll show you the finished *Girl 38*, if you tell me about your and Mila's adventure.'

Her eyes narrowed as she considered my proposal.

'I think it is a good deal,' she said. 'But I wonder if you will be interested. I can see that you live in the present and the future,' she said, tapping my exercise book, 'and my story – it is in the past.'

'I like hearing about the past,' I told her truthfully, and she raised her grey eyebrows in surprise.

'Well, when would you like to hear the first part? You see, it's not a story that can be told all at once.'

'Tomorrow, here at the same time? Or maybe half an hour later?' I was sure that Lena wouldn't even notice that I was gone.

'It's a "date", as they say,' she told me, and her face once again creased up with happiness.

THREE

Julius couldn't have been more different from the image that I'd built in my head if he'd tried. I felt immediately guilty that I'd thought of him as a Vilk.

But when he appeared at the front of our class next morning, I wished I'd caught a photo of him, so that I could use it as a basis for future drawings. He had very light, white-blond hair and incredibly long legs. He stood as if poised to leap into the air.

Weirdly, he didn't seem bothered about standing in front of a class of people he didn't know. 'Hi, I'm Julius,' he said simply, smiling at all of us.

'Welcome, Julius,' said Mr Kim, springing into action. 'Everyone, this is, well… this is Julius. He's joining us from Shetland. Anyone know where that is?'

Julius seemed to like the question and looked around, his left eyebrow raised. I got the impression that he found a lot of things amusing.

'It's an island in Scotland,' said Gem in a bored voice, without raising her hand or even looking up from her homework diary. Her black fringe covered her eyes so that I couldn't tell what her expression was. I guessed that she was secretly intrigued, but pretending not to be.

'Yes, very good, Gemma. Welcome to our…' said Mr Kim, but Julius interrupted, 'Aye, you're close, but not quite. It's an archipelago, a wee group of islands. I come from one of 'em called Yell. It's only got nine hundred and seventy-one inhabitants at the last count, and there were thirty-three of us in my school. We have a huge otter population, though. Apparently there are ten times as many otters on the island as there are people. It's mad, eh?'

He sounded friendly, as if he wanted to sit down and have a chat about his life, but I could feel Gem spiking up, like an angry hedgehog. She grabbed a strand of her hair and began to furiously twirl it around her finger. Julius didn't realise it, but he'd just done the worst thing possible – he'd made Gem look stupid in front of the whole class.

'Oh, yes, of course – Yell,' said Mr Kim. 'You're going to have to tell us more about it. Maybe in our next form period. For the moment, could you sit here?' He pointed to a seat at the front of the class, next to Arun, who gave him a thumbs-up. Arun has loads of friends, but likes his own space. That's why, wherever possible, he tries to avoid sitting next to anyone. I wondered if he would be bothered by Julius being thrust upon him, but he grinned and moved his books along to make space for his new desk mate.

Although Julius's entrance had been awkward, I thought things might improve as the day went on. But, as it turned out, his trouble was that he just didn't have any sense of danger – in fact, he seemed to plough straight into the riskiest situations. He should have kept his head down for a few days, at least until he'd sussed who in the class he should watch out for. If he'd read *Girl 38,* he would have seen Gem as Hawk Eye, complete with exclamation marks around her head and a floating 'STOP' sign, to ward off anyone who thought that they could cross her. But he hadn't, so I suppose he had no real way of knowing how bad she could get.

We had hockey first thing and Julius's sports kit was nothing like the rest of ours. He was wearing high-top basketball-style trainers, like the kind that you see in old films, and instead of the red sweatshirt with the school logo, he had a huge one in deep crimson that said, 'Angus's Fish Bar' in swirly writing. His parents hadn't got round to buying the proper kit yet. His jogging bottoms were too short and he'd hitched them even higher to reveal his shins. He paraded around the courts swirling his hockey stick like a Victorian gentleman.

Dilly, Ruby and I cracked up because he was being so ridiculous, and Gem looked daggers at us. She was in the middle of telling us about her latest time in the swimming try-outs, and we clearly hadn't been concentrating. Julius was already beginning to steal attention away from her.

But then we had biology and that was where the turning point came. Biology is Gem's best subject and she's far and away the top of the class. We'd been learning the major organs of the body and had been given a project for homework – we had to choose an organ to make out of household stuff, complete with labels for the various elements. I'd made a heart out of blue tack and pipe cleaners, showing the different arteries. It wasn't my best effort, but I'd got a bit carried away with *Girl 38* and run out of time to do anything better. Dilly made a stomach out of jelly and Ruby had a miniature model of a kidney with veins drawn on to a kidney bean using a silver pen. I thought that was cheating as she hadn't actually created anything new, but she went on and on about how she'd had to use a magnifying glass to make sure that everything was precise.

Gem had gone above and beyond anything that anyone else had come up with. She'd created a human torso out of two kitchen aprons, one on top of the other. The top one was cut in half down the middle and formed the 'skin' layer of the body. When you pulled it apart, you could see all of the main organs beneath. The heart was made of carefully cut up red foil tops, the lungs were pink balloons, the stomach was spray-painted cotton wool, and there were even old bicycle tyres that formed the small and large intestines.

'That's incredible, Gemma,' said Mrs Henley as we gathered round. 'I've never seen this level of detail before. It must have taken you ages.'

'Oh, I enjoyed it,' said Gem, shrugging her shoulders. 'When you know what you're doing, it takes no time at all.'

'It's grand,' Julius agreed, leaning over the model, a bit too close for Gem's liking. 'But can you actually blow up the lungs?'

'How do you mean? They're balloons, and I've already blown them up so they're to scale.'

'Ah, it's a shame that you can't blow 'em up further,' said Julius, sounding genuinely regretful. 'My uncle got me and my brother to help out on his farm in the school holidays. He slaughtered sheep for meat and would have to remove the organs. I saw heaps of sheep lungs and he once let me blow into one of 'em so that we could see how the air moved in and out through the different valves.'

'Ugh, that's the grossest thing I've ever heard,' said Gem. She was right – it *was* gross, but at the same time fascinating. I looked around and could see everyone staring at Julius, probably thinking exactly the same as me.

'You actually blew into one of the lungs?' asked Arun. 'Are you mental?'

'Aye, I was interested. It rose and fell, as if the sheep was still alive,' said Julius.

'What did it look like?' somebody asked. 'Did it smell?'

And then there was a whole flurry of questions about Julius's uncle's sheep's lungs, and nobody paid any attention to Gem's model. It took Mrs Henley ages to calm us down and get us to sit in our seats.

'He just won't shut up,' Gem whispered in my ear. I could tell she was furious.

At the end of the lesson, the four of us got together and I already knew what was coming.

'He's going to have to pay,' she said. 'I'm going to make sure that he pays.'

'What will you do?' I asked. I followed her gaze. She was staring straight at the aquarium in the corner of the lab. I knew it well, because I'd helped to clean it one lunchtime as part of detention for being late three mornings running. It was filled with possibly the most disgusting creatures in the world ever – maggots. They were there as part of a Year Eleven project into how species multiply under different conditions. The aquarium was divided into four sections. One of them had the heat turned up higher, one was pitch black, one was filled with UV lights and the final one had a layer of water at the base.

'Meet me here at lunch,' Gem told us. 'We have work to do.'

+ . . . + +
+ . . +
+

I could still see the look on Julius's face as I walked out of school that day. It was as if it was imprinted on the inside of my eyelids. The thing that had surprised me most was that he thought it had been an accident – that it was actually possible for those maggots to have crawled into his battered rucksack by pure chance. He must have lived a very different life on his little island.

It took a good few seconds for it to sink in that somebody had done it deliberately. It was only his first day at school and somebody already hated him enough to put horrible little slimy creatures in among his books and pens.

When that dawned on him, he looked around the classroom again and his eyes met mine. I could feel the heat rise in my face (I've never been good at hiding anything) and I could have sworn that he knew I'd done it. I had no idea how he'd worked it out, but he had.

It wasn't me! I wanted to shout at him. *Don't make me feel guilty!*

It *had* been me, though. I'd hated doing it, but Gem never did her own dirty work. Dilly and Ruby gathered the maggots from the dark corner of the aquarium. Gem figured that if we took it from this section, it would take everyone longer to realise that they were missing. It was revolting – they had to scoop them out using a sheet of paper and put them in Dilly's lunchbox, as they couldn't find any other containers in the lab. Despite all this, I would have much preferred to do that than the task that

Gem had allocated to me – to empty them into Julius's bag.

'You'll do a better job than either of them,' she whispered to me. 'You're more secretive and that's why you'd make a much better detective. I can trust you.'

I knew that I couldn't say no when she'd said that, so I took the box and crept up to Julius's desk before the others had come back from the canteen. I opened it, and scooped them out into his navy rucksack with Dilly's yoghurt spoon. It was done in an instant, but I spent most of the next ten minutes thinking that one of them must have escaped and was crawling up my arm.

We sat at our desks as if nothing had happened, and watched Julius as he opened his bag to put his lunchbox back in. We waited for the scream. Out of the corner of my eye, I could see Gem's satisfied smirk, but then something happened which I don't think any of us had expected. Julius grabbed a metal tin from his desk, opened it, and emptied out the pens and pencils inside. Then he picked up all the maggots with his bare fingers and put them in the tin. He did it so quickly that only a couple of people noticed what was going on. What was most incredible was that he didn't even squirm once.

'Do you know where these might have come from?' I heard him ask Arun, who was peering into Julius's bag with a mix of disgust and fascination.

'Erm, probably the biology lab, mate. That's grim, though – I can't believe someone did that. D'you want me to come with you to put them back?'

'Cheers, but I'll be OK.'

Within moments he'd disappeared with the tin. Just like that. No fuss, no drama. A part of me wanted to shout with delight that he hadn't caused a huge scene and hadn't let Gem win, but then I caught the look on his face when he came back into the classroom. It was as if something inside him had changed, as though somebody had turned out the light from behind his eyes. It was horrible to see.

FOUR

I was still thinking about that look when I reached home and I suddenly felt I couldn't bear to sit in my room on my own until Mum and Dad came back. I quickly reversed, before Lena saw me through the window. Then I sent her a text saying that I was visiting our neighbour and I turned towards Ania's door instead.

But when I'd walked halfway down her garden path, I hesitated. What if she didn't want to see me? Maybe she'd just offered to tell me her story yesterday because I'd pestered her so much? Then again, we had arranged a 'date', so not coming would be rude of me. I decided to knock, but to be careful that I didn't outstay my welcome.

When the door swung open, any doubt that I

had about her wanting to see me disappeared. Ania smiled and beckoned me in. She was wearing a dress in an unusual design that made it look as if it was splattered with paint, and there was a string of pearls around her neck. She was holding a walking stick, which had a colourful head in the shape of a parrot.

'He helps me out on bad-knee days,' said Ania, motioning to the parrot. 'These days sometimes creep up with no warning.' Then she looked up at me and I saw that her eyebrows were furrowed with worry.

'Am I interrupting you?' I asked her. 'Maybe you need to rest? I can come back another time.'

'No, not at all. I just think to myself that you look sad. Am I right?' Her tiny hand squeezed my shoulder.

'Oh, erm… yes, I suppose. Sort of. I don't want to talk about it.'

I made a point of looking around the room instead. Yesterday, from the conservatory, I hadn't got a sense of what her house was like, and I was surprised that the other rooms were much less tidy. In the living room, every nook and cranny was rammed with stuff. There were huge rickety bookcases on every wall, even in the corridor outside. As I looked closely, I could see that all the books were arranged alphabetically. There was order in the mess.

In the few spaces where there were no books, people in black-and-white photos stared at me, some serious, others smiling. A dark green velvet sofa stood at one end of the room filled with cushions shaped like animals – an elephant, a dog and a giraffe. Next to the giraffe, a familiar ginger hairball was curled up.

'Polish tea?' Ania asked, smiling. 'Oh, yes, it is Chester,' she said, following my gaze. 'I know his name from his tag,' she explained. 'Before I read it, I was calling him "Albert", after my grandfather. He also had ginger hair and a grumpy personality. Chester sometimes comes here during the day. I hope you don't mind. I once left my top window in the kitchen open and he climbed through it. Then I think he decided he liked spending a little time with me, so he comes to visit every now and then. I usually make sure that I send him back out so he'll be with you when you come home from school. I don't keep him for too long, I promise.'

'That's all right.' I didn't mind, but I could hear Gem's voice in my head saying, *She's even trying to steal your cat.*

Within minutes, Ania had put two steaming cups on the coffee table and had taken out an old oil-paint set to examine the different colours that it contained. The shakiness in her fingers seemed to lessen as she handled them.

My question burst out of me before I could stop it: 'Have you ever had a friend who persuaded you to do stuff, even if you didn't want to?'

She looked up, surprised.

'Hmm… let me think. When I was your age… well, I was quite – what's the word? Bold? Strong-willed? – if anything, I was probably the one who encouraged my friends to do things that they didn't want to do. I often regretted it later. But I suppose I always told myself that I was doing it for the right reasons.'

'What sort of stuff?'

'Well… you remember the girl in the painting? Mila? She was my best friend. She was always so shy and quiet. She wouldn't stand up for herself. There was a time, for example, when she was accused by the village shopkeeper of stealing apples from the store. She hadn't done it. She would never do anything like that, but he had his reasons to choose her as the scapegoat. Later the crate of apples was found. It just hadn't been taken off the delivery cart yet. He apologised, but I still wanted to teach him a lesson. One day, I saw that he'd left his new white bed linen to dry out in his front yard. It was a silly thing to do, as it was the middle of winter and the night frost had made the sheets rock-solid. I persuaded Mila to come with me and punch holes in them. You could put your fist through and make a hole because of how hard they were. He was so angry because they looked like Swiss cheese by the time we were done with them.' She chuckled to herself.

'Why did he use her as a scapegoat?'

'It's because she was of Jewish heritage. At the time, there was a lot of suspicion about anyone Jewish, even if they were not practising Jews. Mila's family actually went to our local church, they were more Catholic than Jewish, but it made no difference to those who decided that they hated her. A lot of people in my village did not like what was happening in their world, and they wanted someone to blame, you see. I said that I would not join them, so they turned against me too.'

'Is that why you jumped from the train?'

She thought about my question.

'You could say so. But there is a lot more to that story.'

There was something in Ania's words that soothed the awful hammering of guilt in my chest, and I wanted her to continue talking to me. I needed to escape, if only for a short while, from the horrible present.

'Will you start from the beginning?' I asked her.

And she did.

'It was a world very different to this one. I lived in a small village where all the locals were friends and everyone knew everyone else's business. We were a long way from the nearest town, and there were no cars or telephones. Most of the roads near to my house were dirt tracks in between huge fields, each filled with different crops. When I walked home from the high street, I would see men and women at work, their scythes swinging like butterfly wings.

'Where this story begins, I was a bit older than you. I had turned fourteen and I started to think about what I was going to do when I finished school. I suppose that most girls after they graduated would start looking for a husband, but I wanted to do something more exciting. I promised myself that I would move to a big city and get my own little house and become an art teacher. I think I realised even then that being an artist would not make me very much money, so I would have to teach. You see, I did not want to be dependent on anybody. I decided that I would make my own way. The only person that I badly wanted to come with me was Mila. I always imagined that we would do everything together.'

I tried to picture Gem and me living and working together in ten years' time. Maybe we just weren't the kind of friends that Ania and Mila were.

'As I told you earlier,' Ania continued, 'some people were suspicious of Mila because of her origins, and that included many of the children in our class. They'd been told by their parents that Jewish people brought trouble with them, and they decided to remind her about this at every opportunity. They would sing songs about how she was a horrible germ-ridden thief.

'None of it was true, but they believed it. I am sure that the taunting was worse, because the bullies could see that she was so intelligent and interesting – she always had views about even the most boring things. She had to put up with it for years, but at least it was nothing more than taunts. That was, until *that day*. I later wondered whether Mila knew something terrible was going to happen, because she seemed different for about a week before.'

'Different how?'

'A bit quieter, more scared. The night before that day, she didn't return my signal. Our gardens were opposite each other, and although our houses were a short distance away, I could see the window of her bedroom. We would often send messages to each other in Morse Code using candles and pieces of card that we had painted black. We studied the code from a book and we became very good. I tried to signal to her several times that night, but there was no response. I wasn't worried, because sometimes her mother would tell her off for staying up too late, and we had to cut our Morse-Code conversation short. I thought that we would get to pick it up again next day.

'As it turned out, there wouldn't be another conversation, because next day everything changed.'

I waited for her to carry on, but she was looking beyond me, through the windows that opened on to the front garden. She seemed lost in thought, in another place.

'I have to go,' I told her gently, 'but I'll come back very soon, if that's OK?'

'You know where to find me,' she said, smiling.

FIVE

Mum and Dad were home moments after me. Lena didn't tell them that I'd only just come back, probably because she was scared that she'd be told off for not keeping an eye on me. She didn't know them very well yet, because they wouldn't have minded. In fact, I told Dad straightaway about Ania.

'She's a lovely lady,' he said, pouring himself a drink. 'I can't believe you haven't had a chance to speak to her before.'

'I know, but I am now, and she's telling me her story.'

'Her story?'

'Of what happened to her and her best friend when she was young.'

'I see. What sort of a story is it?'

'I'll let you know when I've found out,' I promised him. 'I have a feeling it'll be incredibly exciting.'

'How ya hanging, Katty?' Mum asked, ruffling my hair as she sat down to eat. We have this thing going where Mum pretends she's 'down with the kids' and speaks in the way she thinks me and my friends do, except they're all weird phrases that she's probably heard on some old American TV show. We both laughed.

'You know, same as always,' I told her, although this wasn't strictly true. 'There's a new boy in our class. His name is Julius. He's a bit strange, but in a good way.'

'Julius? Sounds a bit grand,' said Dad. 'Like Julius Caesar.'

'Yeah. Well, if you'd met him, I don't think you'd say that he's very grand. And he's just moved from some little village up on a Scottish island. Gem hates him.'

'Oh, she does, does she?' Dad asked, raising an eyebrow. 'I bet I can guess why. Is it possibly because he's better than her at something? Or that he's a kinder person and not only interested in himself? Because I think that's probably not difficult.'

'Stop it, Stephen. The poor girl's not nearly as bad as you make out,' Mum said.

Ever since I'd met Gem, Dad had told me I should stand up to her. But it wasn't as easy as he thought. Gem had always been nice to me, and there were many people she wasn't nice to. I didn't really have a choice. It was a weird kind of friendship, but I always thought that in her own way, she looked out for me. That was, at least until we got to Marley High.

My phone started to ring before Mum had finished eating. She nodded that it was OK if I answered it. It was Gem.

'Right, I have a plan.'

'A plan for what?' I asked, although I could guess.

'That idiot didn't care about the maggots. He probably had loads of them in the hovel he lived in before. I've decided that we need to go bigger and I've come up with a great idea. We're going to get him to dress up as even more of a fool than he actually is. You know we have Own Clothes Day for charity?'

'Yeah. That's always in January, isn't it? We only do it once a year, remember?'

'Duh. *I* know that, but he doesn't. We could tell him anything and he'd believe it. He has no idea how things are run in our school. In fact, I thought we'd make it better than Own Clothes Day. We'll give it a theme to make him look even more stupid. I was thinking we'd tell him that he has to dress up as a character from his favourite film.'

I knew that I would be expected to play some sort of part in this and I was about to be told what. I desperately tried to think of some reason why her idea wouldn't work, but I could tell from the tone of her voice that any protests were already too late. I was right.

'I've written a letter to give to him,' she announced. 'I've shown it to Dilly and she agrees that it's super convincing. I've based it on other parents' letters we've had and now I need your help with getting the signature on to the bottom of it, and the school logo at the top. You know I'm rubbish at stuff like that. I'm going to email it to you now. Just print it out and bring it in tomorrow, yeah?'

And she finished the call before I'd even had a chance to respond. Even if she hadn't, it wouldn't have made a difference, as I never would have argued with her. I was pretty certain that she was asking for my help not because she couldn't work out how to add the graphics, but because it was a way of making sure that she wasn't found holding the letter. I would bring it into school tomorrow and if anyone got caught red-handed, it would be me.

I sat on the stairs, still staring at my phone. This idea of Gem's was worse than anything she'd come up with so far. At least with the maggots, only Arun and a couple of the others had noticed what had happened. Here, our whole class, maybe even the whole school, would see Julius being humiliated. It wasn't fair. Nobody deserved that.

I frantically searched for a way of scuppering the plan. I could call her back and tell her that our printer wasn't working or that Mum needed the computer so I wouldn't be able to do it. But the trouble with Gem is that she's known me for so long she can see through any of my lies.

Eventually, I gave up, as I always did. I went into my parents' bedroom and sat at the laptop. I knew that they wouldn't be using it for at least another hour, so I logged into my emails. The whole thing took me less than ten minutes. I scanned in an old letter, copied over the relevant bits, then put them together with Gem's text and printed it.

What made it even worse was that Gem had signed the letter from Mr Kim – lovely, wonderful Mr Kim. I could just imagine what he would think of me if he found out that I was involved in this.

Dear Parent/Guardian,

I am writing to remind you that on Wednesday we will be running an Own Clothes Day with a twist – we would like to encourage pupils to dress up as their favourite film character, all in the name of charity. The standard donation for taking part will be £2 per pupil, but we do welcome larger sums, should you wish to give more. There will be prizes for the most exciting costumes, so we encourage everyone to be as imaginative as they can.

We do hope that an enjoyable day will be had by all.

Kind regards,
Mr Elliot Kim
8K Form Teacher

'Did you bring it?' asked Gem, the moment she saw me in our classroom next morning.

I nodded and tried to pass her the envelope, but as I predicted, she indicated that I should keep it.

'It's going to be awesome!' whispered Dilly, rubbing her hands together. 'I can't wait to see everyone's faces when they see him. I wonder what freaky character he'll choose. I hope he embraces it.'

Gem herself loved any opportunity to dress up. At her last birthday, she decided to have a superhero theme and went as Wonder Woman, complete with a red-and-gold corset and a shield. She looked awesome, but not quite as awesome as Dilly, who came as Catwoman in a shimmering bodysuit and mask that she'd made herself. Everybody loved her costume, apart from Gem, who'd hated the attention that Dilly was getting. For the next week or so, she'd hardly spoken to Dilly, who got more and more upset and couldn't figure out what she'd done wrong. I'd wanted to go as Girl 38, complete with wild, combed-back hair, a bow and arrow, and long, silver moon boots. But nobody would know who I was, so I chose Batgirl instead.

We agreed that we'd wait until just before the last lesson to leave the letter on Julius's desk – that way, we'd minimise the chance of him speaking to anyone about it.

The envelope was hidden in the pocket of my blazer. I kept putting my hand in to check that it was still there, paranoid that I'd dropped it. I couldn't concentrate on anything that day, not even *Girl 38*. The only thing looping through my mind was how much I didn't want to be involved in the whole thing.

We had a double period of history with Miss Seymour before lunch and Julius sat in the seat in front of us. Did he not realise how close he was getting to the enemy? I stared at the back of his head and wished that I could telepathically transmit a message to him, telling him to ignore the letter that he was about to receive and to steer as clear of Gem as he possibly could.

'Right, everyone, we're going to do an introduction to World War Two this term. We'll begin by looking at the political situation in Europe in the late 1930s, which led to the start of the war in 1939, but before that, let's brainstorm everything you know about the Second World War, because I'm sure that a lot of you will be quite well-informed on the subject already. Put up your hands and I'll jot down any thoughts that you have.'

History was Gem's least favourite subject. She still did well at it – she did well in everything – but it didn't interest her. 'What's the point of learning about the past?' she said once when she was at mine for dinner. 'It's over and done with. It's not like the exact same things are ever going to happen again.

We should move on and start talking about stuff that might actually be useful to us in the future.'

Dad had rolled his eyes. Then, even though I shot him a warning look, he said, 'We're constantly moving forward *because* of the past. It forms the ingredients of the future. We need to learn from our mistakes and our successes. Every single thing that we use today, from a tablet to a car, was invented and improved by people over the course of history through trial and error. We owe everything to our forefathers, Gem. We literally wouldn't be here without them. And you want to write them off, just like that, because you're bored by them?'

I could tell that she hated being told off by Dad, but she pretended that she didn't care by shrugging her shoulders.

Today, with Miss Seymour, she was showing that she knew her stuff, but it was obvious that she was thinking about more exciting things. Further plans to get at Julius.

'It lasted from 1939 to 1945,' she said, with a mildly-bored expression on her face. 'There were two opposing military alliances – the Allies and the

Axis. Britain was on the Allied side and Hitler on the Axis side, along with Mussolini. The war involved more than thirty countries and it included the first use of nuclear weapons in history.'

Gem continued to reel off the facts as if from an encyclopaedia, so rapidly that Miss Seymour could barely keep up with writing them on the board. Eventually, she stopped her halfway through a sentence and said, 'Thank you, Gemma. Anyone else?'

Julius raised his hand.

'My great-grandfather was in the navy – he fought in the Battle of Narvik in 1940. We won that battle, but his best mate died when he was hit by a shell. He was sad about it for ages. He always told me how much he missed him, even though it was, like, eighty years ago.'

'Yes, this is true,' Miss Seymour agreed. 'We must remember that while learning historical events and facts is important, it's the human experiences that form them which are often the most fascinating. We're lucky enough to have many recorded stories of World War Two survivors, and we're organising a trip to the National Archives, where you'll be able to do your own research into many incredible experiences. Julius, if your great-grandfather is feeling up to it, perhaps you could also record an interview with him, and we could play it to the class?'

'Aye, I reckon he would have loved to do an interview,' said Julius, grinning at the thought. 'But he died three years ago now. I could tell you some of his stories, though – I've written 'em all down so that I don't forget 'em.'

I could see Gem scowling. *'I've written 'em all down,'* she imitated under her breath in a Scottish accent. 'What a *wee* creep.'

'There'll definitely be an opportunity for you to tell us more about him,' Miss Seymour promised. 'But today we're going to talk about what led to the outbreak of war, and then I'm going to get you started on a project that we'll be working on until half-term.'

At the end of the lesson we were split into five groups, each of which would research a different Second-World-War topic. I could see Gem looking around to see who might join our foursome, when Miss Seymour started allocating everyone numbers.

'I want to mix up the groups so you don't work with people that you always sit with.'

I ended up in the fours – the same group as Julius, and we were set the task of researching everyday life in Britain during the war. We were given some primary and secondary sources to read over the coming weeks, and the school trip would help too.

'Hey,' said Julius on the way out of the classroom. 'I'm glad we got that topic – it'll be ace to research, eh? I'm interested in what life was like back then. I wish I had a time capsule…'

But he didn't have time to finish, because Gem yanked me away down the corridor. I tried to shoot him an apologetic look, but I'm not sure he saw it.

'What are you doing talking to that idiot?' Ruby asked, as we walked to lunch.

'I wasn't… he was the one who started talking to me.'

Gem didn't say anything, but I could sense that she was prickling up. The red spot on her cheek was practically glowing.

At lunch, we sat at our usual table and planned our strategy.

'Right, so we're going to go to the form room in about ten minutes. Ruby – you and Dil will stay in the corridor, pretending you're chatting, and watch to see if he's coming. If there's any sign of him, ring my phone. Understand?'

They nodded. Gem never asked anybody whether they would mind doing something. She just gave orders.

'I'll go in with Kat. If there's anyone in the room, I'll distract them while she puts the letter on his desk. Easy peasy, right? It'll be over in a few minutes.'

Except I didn't feel that it would be easy peasy. I wished beyond anything that I could have my own Infiniship to speed me away, so that I wouldn't have to play a part in Julius's humiliation. When we got to our classroom ten minutes later, my hands were so sweaty in my pockets that I was making the envelope damp. I was certain that we were going to be discovered.

SIX

I prayed for the room to be empty, but as luck would have it, Arun was there with his mates, Jace and Freddie. They were watching a film on one of their phones, which was playing some pumping music. Arun was laughing and tapping the table with his palm in time to the beat. True to her promise, Gem sprang straight into action.

'What are you watching?' she asked in the special voice that she reserved for Arun.

She blocked their view of me with her back and I quickly sneaked over to Julius's desk. His bag, which only yesterday had been swarming with maggots, was sitting by his chair, almost as if he had left it there in the expectation that it would be filled with something else horrible. *Do your worst,* it seemed to say.

I put the letter on his desk, tucking it under his pencil tin, and then joined Gem, as if nothing had happened. There was not a teacher in sight. My heart slowed its frantic beat.

Half an hour later, at afternoon registration, I saw Julius pick up the envelope, open it, scan the contents and smile. A look of excitement crossed his face. Luckily, at that moment, Mr Kim started talking about parents' evening, and then we had to rush off to our final period, so there was no chance for him to ask any questions.

If he didn't talk to anyone about it throughout double maths, we'd have got away with it. Well – until tomorrow.

I walked out of school, relieved that we'd made it. Gem gave me a secret high-five as we said goodbye to each other outside the school gates. I couldn't believe that it had worked out exactly as planned and I was looking forward to putting it to the back of my mind when I visited Ania. But then I crossed the street and there he was, waiting at my bus stop, swinging his huge, geeky rucksack from side to side.

He smiled when he saw me, and I turned around to see whether the smile was meant for someone else. Surely he wasn't going to try to talk to me again after I'd ignored him in history. Plus, he had obviously suspected that I'd had something to do with the maggots.

But I was wrong. The smile *was* for me. How gullible could he be? I felt like giving him a shake and telling him that he couldn't just think that everyone was his friend.

'Hey,' he said. 'What bus you taking?'

'The 40.'

'I'm getting the 73. I live on Jupiter Close, near the swimming pool. We've moved into my grand-parents' house. It's all tall and thin – it looks like a weird rocket, ready for take-off.'

I laughed awkwardly.

'So, what do you think of school so far?' I asked, when he didn't say anything else.

He looked at me hard then, as if he was considering

something, but at the last moment he changed his mind.

'It's all right. People seem nice. Most of 'em anyway.'

'Yeah.'

'Who you goin' as tomorrow?' he asked suddenly, catching me off guard.

'Tomorrow?'

'For Own Clothes Day. We're supposed to be coming as our favourite film characters, aren't we?'

'Yeah, course. I, erm… I haven't decided yet. You?'

'Don't know. So many great ones to choose from. It's all a bit last minute 'cause I didn't know about it 'til today. Maybe E.T., but I don't know if I'll have a chance to put a proper costume together. It's grand that this school does dressing up too. We did it a lot in my school in Yell, but then again, we were such a wee place that we kinda made our own rules. I wonder who Arun will go as?'

By this point, I was certain that my face was betraying me.

My shoulders slumped with relief when I saw the number 40 bus approaching.

'I've got to go,' I mumbled and almost ran through the opening doors.

'See you tomorrow,' said Julius. 'Can't wait to see who you come as!'

As the bus set off down the road, my heart did its horrible trick of speeding up so much that I felt dizzy. I fell into the nearest seat and shut my eyes. I fought the urge to press the emergency stop and run after Julius, telling him that it was all a lie – a mean, stupid lie – which wasn't even my idea. But I didn't.

And then it occurred to me that because of our conversation, he would know for certain that I had something to do with it. Otherwise, why would I have played along with what he was talking about?

I was so busy worrying about this when I got off the bus to walk the last stretch home that I didn't notice Ania until she called my name.

She was on the other side of the street, panting under the weight of many shopping bags. One of them looked like it was about to slip off the parrot-head. I hurried over.

'I went to the art supply store, Katherine. They had all these beautiful brushes on special offer, so I decided to treat myself, as they say. And then I got some oil paints, and charcoal, and coloured chalk. Goodness, I think I just do not know when to stop. It was all a bit heavier than I imagined.'

I took half of the bags from her and helped her to her door.

'Are you going to start painting again?' I asked.

'Well, I have to tell you that you've inspired me. There is somebody I want to bring to life. But I need all the right stuff, you see. He wouldn't appreciate it if I didn't put in the effort.'

'Mhm.'

I put the bags down in her hallway and made to leave, but she stopped me with a warm hand on my shoulder.

'What's wrong?' she asked.

'Nothing.'

She gave me a look as if to say that she could tell it was a whole lot more than nothing.

'Stay for a while?'

I hesitated. I didn't feel like talking to anyone, but I realised that with Ania, I maybe wouldn't have to talk.

'Only if you tell me more of your story. I want to know what happened on *the day*.'

'Ah, of course.'

Within minutes, I had made myself comfortable in what I had already begun to think of as my armchair and Ania had emptied her bags, stretched her poor legs, and closed her eyes, to better visualise what had happened.

'That day I saw Mila on the way to church, so I was reassured. We went to church every Sunday back then, with my mother and little brother and sister. My father was the village mayor, and he was usually so tired from work that he didn't come with us. That particular Sunday, at the start of September, it was just the four of us that went to Mass, and I ran in after Mila and her mother, leaving the rest of my family to follow. Everything seemed normal. I remember that it was warm for that time of year; people were out in their summer clothes with no coats.

'I still wonder today whether there was anything that would have given me a clue about what was about to happen. Maybe I could have somehow stopped us from going into the building if I'd been a little more alert; if I'd looked at the people around me, instead of admiring my neighbour's new red dress. I think I'll never know.

'Mass started as it always did, with our old priest standing by the altar and spreading his arms to welcome everyone. But then, all of a sudden, his smile transformed into a look of terror, as there was a shout from behind us. I turned in my seat and saw the soldiers. There were so many of them marching into the building and they surrounded us. The last one slammed the door shut.

'I could hear straightaway that they were foreigners. Some were as old as my father and others quite young. They could have been in their last year at school. The two things that linked them were their navy uniform and their narrowed eyes.

'They made the priest carry on with the Mass, although I could tell that it was the last thing he wanted to do. There was desperation in his eyes as he gave a short sermon and shuffled off to the edge of the altar. I think he was hoping to escape through the back door.

'Then I saw some of the soldiers kneeling

and praying, and a small part of me thought that everything would turn out fine. That they were just there to keep an eye on what was going on and that eventually they would let us go. I even tried to catch the eye of one of the younger lads to reassure myself, but he was having none of it. It turned out that I was *very wrong* about the whole thing.

'One of the taller soldiers at the front of the church, a man with a huge moustache, shouted for us to stand and walk quickly, pew by pew, out of the back door, which he had opened. I could see Mila's shoulders shaking as she walked. Our elderly neighbour, Halina – I suppose she was as old then as I am now – had trouble with her leg and it took her a while to shuffle forward. Her slowness seemed to make the men angry, and I saw one of them remove his rifle and poke the end of it into her back.'

'No! Did he shoot?'

'He only pushed her, thank goodness. But she fell with a horrible, sickening thud. I could hear the sound over and over in my ears for weeks after. I can still hear it now. But, yes, eventually she managed to get up and she was pushed along with the crowd.

'When we finally made it out of the church, there were two tables set up and a soldier was standing in between them, as if he was directing traffic. He was trying to separate the Jews from the 'ordinary folk'. He didn't understand that all the people there were both – they might have been of Jewish background, but they went to our Catholic church, just like everyone else. If he wanted to separate them, he would have to split them down the middle. It made me think of cut-out paper girls and boys being torn in half.

'I could sense that Mila was in danger and I pulled her close to me. I decided that there would be no way that I would allow us to be separated.

'But the soldier had other ideas – he took one look at her and cocked his head, which we soon realised was a sign to another soldier to push both her and her mother into the opposite queue to mine.

'"You can't do this!" I remember shouting. "She has to stay with me!" I ran towards her. I thought that if she absolutely had to go into the other queue, then I would too. But then somebody clamped a hand over my mouth and pulled me away. When

I turned, I was shocked to see that it was my own mother. There was a look of warning in her eyes, and I could tell immediately that she understood a lot more than I did. She was scared.'

Ania still had her eyes closed, but she swallowed hard, like I sometimes did when I was trying to fight back tears. I wanted to go over and put my arm around her, but she started speaking again.

'I wanted to scream when I saw Mila being forced into the back of a cart along with lots of our friends and neighbours. It later turned out that these brutal soldiers had got a list of names of local people who had a Jewish connection. They had a destination in mind for them.

'I tore myself from my mother's grasp when I saw the cart being pulled away by horses, and I ran after it as fast as I could. It moved so fast, though, that my awkward legs had no chance of keeping up. I shouted Mila's name over and over, but I wasn't sure whether she could hear me. And when I realised that there was no way that I was going to reach her, I stopped in the middle of the dusty road and yelled, "Mila! I'll find you. I promise you I'll find you!" I shouted over and over until I had no air left in my lungs and I collapsed in the dirt.'

'Did the soldiers come and get you?' I asked her. My voice shook.

'No, they hadn't even bothered to run after me. They knew that I would have to come back, and I did. I walked to the churchyard sobbing and clutched my mother tight. Although at that stage I had no idea where they were taking Mila, I knew that it was somewhere far and that I probably wouldn't see her again in a very, very long time.

'I was sure that the people in my own queue would be allowed to go free, but I was wrong again. When I reached the front desk, the young soldier I'd tried to make eye contact with in the church gave me a scrap of paper and barked in broken Polish, "Train leaves tomorrow at 10.40 a.m. Be at the station." I remember that I stared at it, not understanding what was happening, until my little brother pulled me away.

'Nobody else in my family was given a ticket. The soldiers took one look at them and told them to step aside, along with other women and younger children who were apparently not useful to them.

'Eventually, they let us go home. I know what you're thinking. I think you will say that I should have thrown that awful scrap of paper in the bin and ignored it. If they were stupid enough to allow me to go home, I was free, wasn't I? But I soon heard that things did not work that way. You see, there were rumours about what happened to people who did not obey orders. Mr Bem, the butcher, said that he heard of a man in the next village who had run away from the soldiers. Later, they burned down his family home and his children were forced to beg in the streets. My parents argued for hours about what we should do. In the end, I was told that I would have to pack my suitcase. We were going to the station the next day.'

I was listening to Ania so intently that I was startled by the sudden knock on the door.

'Hello.' I heard Lena's voice. 'I'm sorry to disturb you. Is Kat here?'

I looked at my phone and saw with shock that it was already half-past six. I had no idea where the last hour and a half had gone.

'Sorry,' I whispered to Ania. 'I'll be back soon.'

As I walked out of the door, I started to think of how petty my situation with Gem and Julius was in comparison to what Ania had been through. I needed to be stronger and, most of all, I needed to stand up for what I believed in.

SEVEN

I wished I could tell Mum that I was sick the following morning, but the trouble with having two parents who are doctors is that they always know when I'm lying, plus they both think I should always carry on unless I'm pretty much dying. So I clambered out of bed and tried to distract myself by thinking of Ania's story instead of the day ahead.

When I got to school, the situation was worse than I'd imagined. I could hear laughter halfway down the corridor as I walked in and the drum beat in my chest started. I tried not to give myself away when I entered the classroom, but I was too curious and, in the end, I looked up.

Julius was sitting at his desk in a fantastic costume which, in a real competition, would have definitely won an award for effort. He wore a pair of cut-off dark green trousers and a pale green shirt that looked as though it had been deliberately mud-stained. Over the top was a long, flowing brown cape with a hood made out of a huge woven sack. When I got closer, I glimpsed his glistening gold ring on a chain around his neck, and the best part – a pair of large, hairy hobbit feet made out of papier-mâché attached to a pair of old trainers.

He was Frodo from *Lord of the Rings*. How had he managed to put it together in one evening? I wondered if he'd spent all night on it.

People had different reactions to his costume. Some were staring at him in disbelief, others laughing, others still were waiting for Mr Kim to come in.

Julius looked puzzled and a tiny bit scared. He reminded me of a fragile bird left out in the cold.

'But... I... I got a letter about dressing up for charity,' he was telling Arun.

'Somebody must have played a prank on you,' I heard Arun reply. 'D'you want me to help you find out who? They're idiots, whoever they are. I would get properly mad if someone did that to me.'

I avoided looking at them and went straight to my seat.

'Stop acting so suspicious,' Gem hissed. She hadn't heard what Arun had said. 'It's worked so well. Even better than I imagined!'

Ruby and Dilly were crying with laughter behind their homework diaries.

Moments later, Julius was standing at the front of the class, still wearing his big hairy feet and being questioned by Mr Kim.

'Why are you wearing a *Lord of the Rings* costume?'

I put my head in my hands. It was over. I knew that he was going to show Mr Kim the letter and say that I'd made him believe that the whole dressing-up thing was true, which meant that I definitely had something to do with it.

But Julius coughed and looked around uncertainly.

'Well?'

'I... I think I got the wrong end of the stick. I thought it was dressing-up day for charity,' he said eventually.

'What made you think that?'

When Julius didn't answer, Mr Kim sighed and continued, 'Is this when you did Charity Day in your old school? Anyhow, we'll discuss it later. Do you have something to change into? Did you bring your school uniform with you?'

'No. I only have my PE kit in my locker.'

'Right. Well, you're going to have to go home to change. You have chemistry next, don't you? I'll tell Ms Giordi that you're going to miss first period.'

And as Julius stood there, bewildered, waiting for Mr Kim to finish the register, I was suddenly reminded of the image of Mila, when Ania said that she'd been singled out for stealing the apples. Neither of them was to blame, and neither was brave enough to stand up for themselves. A part of me almost hoped that Julius would tell them about the letter and our conversation at the bus stop yesterday. I would even own up to doing it. I felt that I needed some sort of punishment for what I'd done, otherwise I wouldn't be able to forgive myself. But instead of saying anything, I sat there, picking a hangnail on my left thumb until it bled, and staring out of the window where two pigeons were circling each other in the playground. I knew I was a coward.

I couldn't concentrate at all throughout chemistry. Then, finally, halfway into the second period, Julius came into the lab in his school uniform, still looking flustered. He apologised for being late, didn't make eye contact with anyone, and sat down in the first empty seat he could see.

For the next couple of days, Julius kept his head down. He hardly spoke in lessons, which was unlike him, and he sat alone at lunchtimes on the corner table, reading a book. He didn't look sad exactly, but it was as if he realised that he couldn't be his real self – he needed to be a toned down, black-and-white version of Julius. It made me feel terrible.

One rainy afternoon, I saw Arun approach Julius's table with two of his mates, and my first thought was that they would probably start having a laugh at him, but they sat down and Arun showed him something on his iPad. Then Julius picked up one of Arun's headphones and they listened to some music together. I couldn't believe that I'd assumed they'd be mean. It turned out that not everyone was like us.

'What's going on there?' asked Gem, peeping round from behind Dilly's back.

'Looks like Arun, Jace and Dave are hanging out with Julius,' I muttered.

'Arun must be doing it for a dare,' said Gem breezily, but I could see that small spot glow red.

'It doesn't matter, Gem,' said Dilly nervously. 'Your plan worked brilliantly. The main thing is that Julius is right back in his box, where he belongs.'

'Exactly, and we must make sure he stays there.'

EIGHT

Uncle Pete and my cousins came to visit at the weekend and we drove to the South Downs, which distracted me from school for a bit and gave me loads of great ideas for scenery in *Girl 38*. I spent ages drawing bush-covered hills and meandering rivers, except I changed the colours. On Planet U, the rivers were a lurid orange from all the lava, and the black hills rose like the backs of sleeping giants.

When we got home, I tried to make more progress on the comic and keep my mind off having to think about the week ahead.

First Mate Hawk Eye and Girl 38 had been travelling through the mysterious land of Planet U for hours, collecting huge berries that fell from the trees, fluorescent mushrooms and anything else they could get their hands on, and which might be edible. They were about to turn home before nightfall, when they spotted the Vilk. He was partly hidden by a sprawling bush, but his piercing eyes were visible through the leaves. 'Shoot him!' Hawk Eye demanded, so Girl 38 raised her bow and arrow. But no matter how she tried, she couldn't pull back the string of her bow. It was as if an invisible force was stopping her.

I tried to sketch Girl 38 with her arm suspended in mid-air, uncertain about what to do next, but everything about her looked wrong. She just wasn't convincing. I made several more attempts, but they were no better. Eventually, I couldn't stand it any longer. I tore out the pages and scrunched them up.

I stared absent-mindedly out of the window and spotted Ania leaving her house with her shopping trolley. She made her way slowly down the path, and before reaching the gate, she almost tripped over an overgrown bush. She managed to catch the gate-post to steady herself.

I jumped up and ran to the garage to get the lawnmower. I'd never cut the grass for her as I'd promised. Dad showed me how to use the mower when he first bought it, and I'm a pro. I love the smell of cut grass – it reminds me of summer holidays at Uncle Pete's. I figured that I wouldn't have time to prune all of Ania's bushes, but I could at least get rid of the dangerous branch and cut the grass.

First I snipped away at the worst bits of the offending bush. Then I pulled the lawnmower through the hole in the fence and I was off. I'd forgotten how efficient it was, because by the time Ania was back half an hour later, I'd made a good start in the jungle.

I laughed when I saw the delight on her face. She looked so pretty, standing there on the sunny patio.

'Katherine, it looks fantastic. You're my saviour!' she shouted over the hum of the mower.

'I'll do the front for you later this week,' I said, wiping my forehead.

'You don't have to. It's the back garden that I wanted to use the most. Now I can bring my friend out into the sunshine,' she said. 'The light is so much better here than indoors. I've been secretly waiting to take him outside for ages.'

'Who's your friend?' I asked, confused. I wondered if she meant Chester.

'I'll introduce you to him, if you could help me with one last thing?'

She led me back to her easel. The picture of Mila had been removed and carefully leaned against the wall. In its place, there was another small canvas – the beginnings of a new piece of work. It was a painting of a man with light-coloured hair and an impressive beard. He was peering at something in the distance, a look of concentration on his face.

Together, we took the easel into the garden, along with a stool and a sun chair, both of which had been gathering dust in Ania's cupboard under the stairs.

'Who is he?' I asked, when we'd positioned everything in the sunniest spot.

'I've named this painting "The Good Soldier". He is somebody who helped me at a time when I needed it most. It was you who inspired me to paint him, by asking me to tell you my story.'

I peered at the portrait. It was in early stages, but

I could tell exactly what sort of a person this man was. His mouth looked stern, but there was something wonderful about his eyes – something bold and honest. I knew immediately that I would like him if I met him and I wanted to find out more about him.

'Tell me what he was like,' I said, settling myself on the little stool.

'Well, before I introduce you,' said Ania, lying back in the deckchair and smiling, 'I will have to tell you about what happened when I got on the train.'

'I'll ask Mum and Dad if I can have my dinner here and spend the evening with you. My cousins have gone, so I'm sure they won't mind.'

'Great. I will bring my food too. I feel we have a few hours of sunshine left,' she said. 'We might even be treated to a lovely sunset.'

Within minutes I was back with my bowl of spaghetti, ready to be taken away from my own worry-filled life. Ania sighed, closed her eyes and began.

'There were so many people at the station when we arrived. Nowadays, there are crowds everywhere, aren't there? I am sure that you are used to it. But where I lived I had never seen so many people in one place at one time. They were not just from our village, but from the whole local area. Most of them were packed into the station hall, so tightly that they could barely move.

'The strangest thing was, that for such a huge crowd, there was very little noise. It was as if someone had turned off the sound in a film. I think that people were too scared to speak. I saw an old man with white hair hugging a girl of about my age very tight to his chest. He had beautiful dark eyes and there were tears running down his cheeks. That image has stayed with me, you know, because it was so painful and so beautiful at the same time. I tried to paint it once, but I couldn't make it look real.'

'I think you could. You're an amazing painter. You should try again.'

'Who knows? Perhaps I will one day, when I am in the right mood. Anyway, I was stubborn back then and I was determined that I wouldn't cry, even though I wanted to. So I didn't even look my parents in the face when I said goodbye to them. I remember holding my mother as if I never wanted to let go. By then the soldiers had started to usher us on to the train, and we were being pushed in all directions. I got tripped and squashed, but I eventually ended up inside a carriage. I'd never been on a train before. I had no idea how it all worked, or what was about to happen. I had realised at that point that it would be a most unusual train journey.

'There were no seats left. I think the train had come from another village before arriving with us, so there might not even have been any free seats when it arrived. I remember having my suitcase squeezed between my feet and searching for something to hold on to, when I heard a kind voice say, "Come and sit down. I've been sitting for ages, so it's your turn now."

'I looked up and locked eyes with a boy who was probably a couple of years older than me. He had blond hair and freckles, and the build of somebody who spent a lot of time working in the fields. He smiled, and I realised that it was the first smile I had seen that day. Another boy said, "Let me take that." He picked up my suitcase and somehow managed to find a space for it in the rack above our heads. He looked more serious than his freckly friend – maybe it was because of his glasses and his thick wool suit, which looked so uncomfortable. I saw the sweat on his forehead and wondered why he had not even loosened his tie. "I'm Adam," he said, "and this is Henryk."

'Even though I was still scared, the boys made me feel much better. I had guessed correctly that Henryk was a farm lad, and it turned out that Adam was the son of a doctor in a village not far from us. They knew each other from school, but they were as different as they could possibly be. When I arrived in the carriage, they had been arguing over where the train was heading.'

'Where did they think you were going?' I asked her, dreading the answer.

'Henryk thought that the enemy soldiers wanted our people to fight for their army. He kept stamping his feet and saying that he would refuse.

'"Of course they don't want us to fight for them, you fool," said Adam. "Why would they want someone to fight for them who doesn't believe in their cause? I tell you, they're sending us to a labour camp. I've heard about them. They need to produce huge amounts of food to help with the war effort and they grow it on big farms where they work you to the bone. They need ruthlessly efficient workers. And if you're not efficient enough, well... they get rid of you."

'There was a group of younger girls at the other end of the carriage and it was obvious that they were listening, so we lowered our voices. I could tell that the boys didn't want everybody to panic.

'"Why did they choose us?" I asked.

'"Look around you. Everyone here is fit, healthy and young," said Adam. "They think that older adults won't work as fast, and younger children are no use to them, because they wouldn't know what they're doing and they'll probably cry."

'He seemed to know so much about it and I thought perhaps he might be able to help me figure out where Mila was. I told them about what had happened outside the church the day before. Then, as soon as I'd said it, I wished I could take it back.'

'Why? What did they tell you?' I asked Ania. The dread that I'd been feeling reached a new level.

'Adam looked at me strangely. "I'm not sure it's a good idea, you looking for your friend," he said. "Where they're sending us is bad, but where they're sending her is much, much worse. My dad has heard all about it – they've built special villages within cities just for Jewish people. They're separated from the world by high walls and barbed wire and nobody can go in and out. People are dying of starvation, and if that doesn't get them, then disease will. There's a horrible typhus epidemic spreading. It is possible that your friend was sent somewhere else, but I think it's almost certain that she's ended up in one of these places."

'I wanted to clamp my hand over his mouth and stop the awful words. They weren't true. They couldn't be. It sounded like the sort of visions of the future that my father read in the strange books he got from his Russian friend. I thought that Adam had read something similar and was using the ideas to spread fear. I was so mad with him.

'"You're saying it to make us scared. Why would anybody trust you anyway?" I shouted at him, but he looked at me with his eyebrows raised, as if he didn't care that I didn't believe him. It was that look on his face which made me feel sick with nerves, because it made me realise that what he was saying was true, or at least close to the truth.

'I sat for a long time, not looking at either of them, watching the fields changing outside the window. From a distance, I could see the colours that belonged to the different crops – the light yellow of wheat, the gentle gold of barley, the pale green of rye. I spotted the tiny farmers with their scythes working the fields like busy little insects. As the train slowed, I saw the gathering of hay and a group of girls bouncing on top of a sheaf, laughing as an angry man attempted to swat them away.

'I couldn't imagine that somewhere beyond those haystacks and the perfect rows of birches with their leaves rustling in the wind, there were people who had put other people behind a wall and were letting them die, perhaps even *wanting* them to die.'

'That's horrible,' I said. 'But why? Why were they doing it?'

'I was asking myself the same question, Katherine. And I was panicking about what I was going to do.

In fact, I must have panicked out loud, because I remember that the whole carriage turned to look at me.

'Then Henryk, who had been quiet for a long time, whispered something to Adam, who nodded. He put his right hand out to me, grabbed my suitcase with his left, and told me to come with him.

'The three of us pushed through the door of the carriage and down the corridor, which was so filled with people that we must have stepped on hundreds of feet before we got to the doors. There was a cold draught because the windows weren't fully secure, so nobody wanted to sit there if they could avoid it. They would rather be cramped and warm. I wondered if it was the only empty space on the whole train.

'"What are you doing?" I hissed at them. "Why did you bring me out here? It's freezing!"

'"We have a plan," Henryk said. "But you need to promise us first that even if you don't agree with it, you will not tell anyone about it. You must swear on your friend Mila's life that you won't."

'"I swear."

'I had only just met the two of them, but there

was something in their faces that told me I could trust them and that they belonged to a group of very few people who actually understood, even in some small part, what might be happening to us.

'Nothing could prepare me, though, for what they said next.

'"We're going to jump," said Adam.

'"What?" I thought I'd misheard him, what with the wind that rattled through the carriage and the noise of the train on the tracks.

'"We're going to jump," he repeated. "I've been planning it since I found out yesterday that we'd be on this train. My uncle's a train driver and I know a bit about how they work. They always slow down before they get to their next stop, so the trick is to jump at the right moment."

'"You're mad," I said.

'"No," said Henryk. "What's mad is staying on this train. If we do it right, we'll be fine. We'll survive the jump and we'll be able to get away."

'"And if you don't survive?" I asked him.

'"Well, that's not an option. The only question left is whether you'll jump with us."'

'And you did? You jumped, didn't you?' I asked, my nails digging into my arm.

Ania nodded.

'Adam told me that I had around six minutes to make a decision because that was the distance to the station. His plan was to jump and then escape somewhere to a nearby farm to find work, until it was safe enough to return home.

'"It's your only chance to save yourself and to find your friend," he said. "If you don't take this first step, how are you ever going to make it past the wall to find her?"

'I think, in the end, it was the answer to that question which made up my mind for me.

'"I'll do it," I said with my eyes shut.

'We listened to make sure that there were no soldiers near, then Adam got out his penknife and fiddled with the lock on the door. At first, he struggled and I remember the flood of relief when I realised that the plan might not work – but then there was a burst of wind, as the door suddenly swung open. Adam went first. I watched his feet as he stood there, his hand holding on to the inside wall of the train as he judged the speed. He had been right. I could feel beneath my feet that the steady chugging was getting slower and slower. And then he nodded to signal that it was the right time. I turned to check that nobody had seen what we were doing, and when I turned back, he was gone.

'Then Henryk grabbed my hand tightly and pulled me forward and upwards with all his strength. One moment our feet were still on the dirty wooden train floor and the next we were suspended, caught on a rush of fresh autumn air. In that tiny glimmer of time, I felt light and free, and happy, and then I hit the ground and everything turned black.'

NINE

The night after Ania told me about the train leap, I dreamed that I was jumping through the air, falling off the edge of Girl 38's Infiniship, swirling through space, asteroids and planets spinning around me as far as the eye could see. Strangely, I wasn't scared and that was because I was holding tightly on to somebody's hand. When I looked to my left, I realised that the hand belonged to Julius. He smiled at me and I felt safe.

I remembered my dream the following week when we had our first swimming lesson of the term and were practising diving. I'm terrible at swimming – I struggle to do half a length of breaststroke without getting tired, but at least it meant that we wouldn't have to do anything in groups and I wouldn't even have to talk to anyone for a whole hour.

Gem loves swimming – she's been doing it since she was tiny and she gets super-competitive about it. In primary school she'd topped the league at three junior swimming championships. Then her little brother was born and her mum didn't have the time to take her to swimming club any more, so Gem would try to get me to go to the local pool every Saturday, with my dad driving us both there and back. I went, of course, because it was Gem, but I hated every minute of it, though I insisted to Dad that it was great. Even with floats, I was constantly worrying about being out of my depth and sinking to the bottom.

In our school swimming lessons, Gem would always show off and try to race against the boys, although she knew full well that nobody was as fast as her. She never said it out loud, but her long-term goal was to represent our school in the county championships. Only one girl and one boy were chosen from each year group, and it was currently

Gem and Paul Miller from 8N, who is also insanely good.

Our swimming teacher, Mr Leonard, who we were all a little scared of, separated us into our usual three groups based on ability and speed, and we got into our lanes.

'We'll start off with ten lengths of alternating front crawl and breaststroke as a warm-up,' he said, rubbing his hands together. I made a mental note to use him as a model for my villains in later episodes of *Girl 38*.

'I want you to give me your very best from the outset,' he said. 'Remember – we're aiming for speed, style and…?'

'Stamina,' Gem finished off, slipping expertly into the water. She'd recently saved up her pocket money to buy a special swimming cap which was supposed to help you glide through the water more quickly. Every second counted.

'That's right, Gemma. In you all get.'

'Hi, I'm new,' Julius said, standing at the edge of the pool in his too-big swimming shorts. They were tied tightly at the waist, as if he was making sure that nobody would pull them down. Maybe he'd finally realised that he needed to keep his guard up.

'Ah, yes – Julius, is it? Right. Where do you want to go? The fast, medium, or slow lane? How would you rate your ability?'

'Erm, well, I suppose I can go quite fast,' said Julius.

'Go in the medium lane,' Mr Leonard instructed.

I made sure that I went at the very end of the slow lane, behind Ruby, who is almost as bad as me. Her long legs seem to fly out in all directions when she swims, so I made sure I left a big enough gap before following her. I started my painful attempts at front crawl, but after a few strokes I was already messing up the breathing. I'd done half a length when the whistle blew and Mr Leonard shouted, 'Julius. Move to the fast lane.'

On the second length, I relaxed into the steady rhythm of breaststroke – pull with arms, head up, head down, kick. It would all be OK. Now that Gem had humiliated Julius enough, she would get bored with it. Then, I would hopefully get a chance at some point to say sorry to him and tell him that it was just a joke that was taken a bit far.

I wondered what Ania was doing. Did she spend her days painting, Chester curled up at her feet? Did she read the hundreds of books in her house? Did she daydream about Mila and the things they got up to when she was young? Maybe she wrote letters to her? Some people still do that.

Once, on a school trip to the British Museum, I saw a mummy of a pharaoh who had been buried with a love letter. It was in hieroglyphics and had survived more than five thousand years, rolled up next to his head. I stared at it through the glass of the cabinet and wished that the person who had written it had known that their love had lived on for centuries and was now being seen by visitors from all over the world.

In a world like Girl 38's, there would be no letters. There might not even be email in the way we know it now. Maybe everyone would have little chips inside their arms and messages would be transmitted through these. You'd feel a little zap of electricity on your skin and you'd know someone was communicating with you.

I was still thinking about this when I finally

finished the warm-up and saw that Mr Leonard was ordering everyone out of the pool.

'Come and gather round,' he said. There was an unusual look on his face that I'd never seen before and I realised that it was extreme excitement. His bushy black eyebrows furrowed in a fierce 'V'.

'Julius, stay in the pool, please.'

We stood on the side shivering and stared at Julius, who was clinging on to the edge at the deep end.

My intuition told me that things were about to take a turn for the worse. How did he manage to be constantly singled out? Maybe Gem had done something to set him up without telling us? I imagined her kicking him 'semi-accidentally' so that he collided with somebody swimming from the other direction.

But it turned out that Gem hadn't been involved.

'Everyone, I want you to observe Julius closely as he does two lengths of front crawl. I want you in particular to watch his breathing, his tumble-turn and the way he glides through the water after he kicks off. I think you'll agree that it's impressive. Julius, whenever you're ready…'

We watched as he pushed himself off at the other end of the pool. Mr Leonard started the stopwatch. For the first third of a length only his back was visible as he slid effortlessly through the water, like the eels that Mum always loved watching when we went to the aquarium.

Then he began to kick more vigorously as his head turned from side to side every three strokes. When he reached our end of the pool, he did a quick tumble-turn at a diagonal (like a real professional) and he was off again. It was like watching an Olympic swimmer, except one without a cap and in massive oversized shorts that looked like they belonged to his dad.

'Thirty-five and a half seconds! That's incredible!' shouted Mr Leonard, staring at his watch. I don't think I've ever seen him look so happy.

'Whoop! Way to go!' I turned to see Arun cheering and some of the other boys in our class clapping like mad, and I felt a chill go down my back.

'We've never had anyone in this school who's got anywhere close to thirty-five seconds,' Mr Leonard explained, walking back to where we stood. 'It means that we have a real chance in the championships. Were you in your county team at your old school?' he asked Julius, who I now noticed hadn't even been wearing any goggles.

'Sorry?'

'Surely you must have been in some sort of squad?'

Julius stared at him as if he was speaking a different language.

'I used to swim in the sea in Yell with my brother from when I was wee. He taught me to swim. Then they built the big pool near our school a coupl'a years ago and I went there. Much easier to swim in the pool than in the sea. Far less choppy, and warmer too.'

'You must have had a good coach there?'

'Nah. I just went with my mate, Terry, every Saturday. We'd race each other. He usually won, but the last time I went before I moved down here, I beat him. He might have let me have it, though – you know, because I was leaving.'

'Come and see me at lunch,' said Mr Leonard. 'I think you show great promise. I want to discuss a few things with you.'

A sick drumming of doom started as I slid back down into the water. Julius was going to be chosen for the team. I knew that he was at least five seconds faster than Gem and he wasn't even trying, so he would definitely take Paul Miller's place. Gem would still go to the championships to represent the girls, but Julius would obviously be the star of the show – if Mr Leonard was so ecstatic about his time, he could probably go far. He might not just be the fastest boy in our year, but maybe even the whole school.

A small part of me hoped that Gem might be OK about it. After all, he didn't deliberately try to outshine her. He didn't even know about the championships. But, as I soon found out, this made absolutely no difference – if anything, it made the situation a whole lot worse. And when Gem saw Arun giving Julius an encouraging slap on the back as he walked away behind Mr Leonard, she was madder than I'd ever seen her.

TEN

'I can't believe that little idiot,' she said, glancing at Julius, when we were sitting at lunch later that week. I thought she was referring to what happened at swimming, but she continued, 'He's pretending that nothing's affecting him, although deep down I know it is. He hated the maggots, and he was squirming inside when he was wearing his silly little costume.'

'At least it seems that he didn't tell Mr Kim about the letter,' Dilly observed. She was always scared of getting in trouble.

'You need to do something that will get to him,' said Ruby, picking out the tomato chunks in her salad. She was never hungry and seemed to survive on lettuce leaves. 'I have an idea. I reckon that we could pretend to be a mystery girl who fancies him. He's exactly the type to go for something like that. We can send him lots of subtle messages to show that she's keen and eventually get him to meet with her – he'll get ready for a date with his "mystery girlfriend" and we'll tell him to turn up in a special spot. We'll make sure it's a place where loads of people can see him looking like an idiot when his girl doesn't show up. It'll be perfect. What do you reckon?'

She looked at Gem and I could tell that she was hoping she would love the idea and praise her for coming up with it. She nervously wound one of her plaits round and round her finger. I realised with horror that I probably often had the same look on my face.

Gem chewed slowly, deliberately keeping us waiting.

'It's not a bad plan,' she said. 'I have to have a think about how we can make it more effective, though. But in the meantime, we should definitely get hold of his number. It'll come in useful, I'm sure. Kat, you try and get it over the next couple of days.'

'What? Why me?' I asked, maybe a bit too quickly.

Gem raised her eyebrows at my protest.

'He's already got a thing going on with you. Everyone can see that. He was trying to chat to you after history last week, remember? I even thought he might like you then. You know, properly *like* you, if you get my meaning.'

They cracked up laughing as if it was the funniest thing in the world.

'D'you know what?' Gem continued. 'I think we should actually write the messages from you. He'll think you're well into him and get really excited. Then it'll serve him doubly right when he finds out it's not true. We'll hit him right where it hurts!' she said, chuffed at how quickly she'd come up with it.

A bubble of panicked laughter erupted from my mouth.

'No way. He doesn't like me like that. We should do it from someone anonymous – a mystery girl. It would be much funnier that way.'

'Get the number as soon as you can and let us all know when we're ready to go,' Gem insisted.

'What if I can't?'

I considered telling them about my conversation with Julius at the bus stop to prove that there was no way that he would ever trust me. The only reason I didn't was because I was worried that Gem would have a go at me for revealing that I was involved. If Julius had told the teachers about what I'd said, they would immediately suspect her too, as they knew we did everything together.

'Don't be silly. He'll be so happy for you to ask him for his number. He won't believe his luck.'

'I can't ask...'

But Gem was no longer listening. I could see her eyes wandering across the lunch hall, where Arun and his gang were sitting at one of the far tables, still in their sports kit. They'd just come back from Rugby Club and were high-fiving each other over and over, deliberately drawing attention to themselves.

'We'll get them!' Arun shouted. 'When we go out on that pitch tonight, they won't know what's hit them!'

'What's going on?' Dilly asked.

'They've got the final of the rugby tournament

tonight,' said Gem grimly. 'I reckon they'll win. They're good. Arun's the team captain. Bet he'll be awarded a prize at the Sports' Ball.'

Suddenly, Gem's eyes looked glassy, and she turned away from us. For a moment, I thought that she might be about to cry, but she coughed and hurriedly put a handful of chips into her mouth.

That was when it hit me why she'd mentioned the ball. *She* was supposed to have been the swimming star there, but now everyone's attention (maybe even Arun's) would be on Julius.

'So, you'll get the number tonight?' she said, not looking at me.

'I'll try.'

But when I walked out of school that day, trying to get Julius's number couldn't have been further from my mind. In fact, I'd decided to pretend to Gem that I'd attempted to talk to him but he'd ignored me. In reality, I was going to do everything that I could *not* to bump into him. I even planned to avoid the bus stop and walk home instead. It would take me ages, but I was desperate.

Unfortunately, things didn't turn out that way.

'Hey, wait up!'

My heart sank. Julius was rushing across the road to catch up with me, his hair a moving cloud of white-blond. I kept walking, hoping he might think I hadn't heard, but within seconds, he was next to me.

'Hey,' he repeated, as if nothing had happened. 'How was your day?'

I stared at him. Why wasn't he mad at me? If I were him, I'd be fuming. The cartoon version of me would have little waves of steam coming out of my ears.

'Yeah, not so bad,' I said. 'Yours?'

'Grand,' he said, grinning. 'Been doing some extra training with Mr Leonard. It's awesome about the swimming thing. It made me feel better after last week. I looked like a right prat with the whole dressing-up thing. But I realise it was a joke. It's probably what you guys do to new kids. At the docks near my old school, they did an initiation for new fishermen by knocking them off the boat into the freezing water on their first trip – coat, boots and all. Horrible. One of them ended up in hospital with pneumonia. I got away lucky with the Frodo costume and a wee bit of mocking.'

His accent was stronger than ever when he got excited, and he talked faster than anyone I knew. It was as if his head was buzzing with so much excitement, that he didn't have time to dwell on anything bad that happened to him.

'Well done on the swimming championships. That's cool,' I said, trying to sound enthusiastic. 'It's so hard to get into those. I don't think I would have been able to swim fifty metres in double your time.'

'I bet that's not true. And even if it is, it doesn't matter. I'm sure there's loads of stuff that you're awesome at. I can tell that about you straightaway, and I'm a good judge of people,' he said.

I felt my face heating up, but Julius didn't seem to notice.

'Hey, come round to mine some time?'

'Sorry?'

'My mum keeps saying that I should invite some

of my new mates to our house. It's a pretty big place – it belongs to my nan, but she's not managing quite so well now, so we're here to look after her. I've never lived in a house that big before. In Yell, we just had a wee red farmhouse and that was for the four of us. Now my brother Kit's gone off to uni, Dad's still in Yell and we're here.'

'I'm sorry.' He probably thought that I was talking about his nan, but in my head, those words covered a whole lot more. I wanted to tell him the truth. The confession was there, waiting on the tip of my tongue. I opened my mouth but then clamped it shut again. I couldn't do it.

'She's going to be OK. She'll just need a bit of a hand with things.'

'Do you miss your dad?'

'Aye, a lot – and Kit too, although he's annoying most of the time. But the plan is we'll all be back together at Christmas. It'll be awesome. Anyway, do you reckon you'll come round? Remember – 7, Jupiter Close. It's just off the high street.'

'Erm, yeah. I'll let you know.'

'Will you give me your number?'

I read out my phone number to him, and within a minute I saw a text come through from his phone.

'There, now you have mine too.'

I couldn't believe how quickly I'd succeeded in Gem's task, but instead of feeling relieved, I felt devastated.

'Thanks,' I said. What else could I do? Then, 'I'm walking home today,' I told him as we got to the bus stop, and before he could say anything, I waved goodbye like a maniac and marched down the street at a hundred miles per hour.

ELEVEN

I walked home through the park. I thought it might give me time to think about what to do, but my mind was blank. I picked at another hangnail until a trickle of blood made its way down my finger, all the way to my knuckle. I sucked it. It tasted cold and metallic.

I passed our old nursery, on the edge of the park, next to the huge playground. It was almost empty, but there were two girls who looked around four years old still hanging out on the climbing frame. One was blonde and the other dark-haired. They looked like Gem and me when we were little. Behind the window, to the left of the nursery entrance, I could see the class where we'd met and she'd asked me whether I wanted to be friends.

Things had seemed so much easier then. When did it all get so difficult? I trailed in the direction of home.

'Katherine?' Ania was sitting on the front porch of her house wearing a beautiful printed headscarf. The parrot-headed walking stick lay by her feet. I felt myself instantly relax.

'Hello. What are you doing out here?' I asked her.

'I'm thinking,' she said simply. 'I sometimes like to come out here, think, and watch people walk by. I feel like I can tell a lot about a person from their walk. Sometimes I make up little stories in my head about them. I might see a businessman in a fancy suit and sunglasses and think to myself, *He is an international bank robber in disguise.* And you? What have you been doing?'

'I was thinking too... maybe we could think together?'

'Absolutely. I love thinking with somebody else.'

We sat in silence for a few minutes, but what I really wanted was to hear more of Ania's story. I asked whether she could tell me the next instalment.

As she started to speak, I drifted away from the horrible present, transported into her world.

'You got up to the part when you jumped,' I reminded her.

'So I did. I told you that everything turned black because I lost consciousness, but only for a few seconds. When I came round, I saw two faces leaning over me. I couldn't recognise them at first, and there were voices that came in and out of focus, like a faulty radio transmitter.

'It took a few minutes before the awful pain in my left ankle hit me and I realised that I couldn't move it. Then my mind put together everything that had happened. I remembered the soldiers, the train, the boys, the leap – and I knew that something had gone wrong.

'"We're so far from where we were supposed to be," Henryk kept repeating over and over, and Adam cursed under his breath. It turned out that we'd jumped much earlier than we should have done and that we were nowhere near any form of civilisation.

'"We need to get to the main road," Adam said. "Then we can flag someone down."'

'But you couldn't find anyone?' I guessed.

'We couldn't even find the road. We walked and walked. I felt guilty because I was slowing them down, hobbling on my ankle. After a few hours, the pain was so bad that the boys had to carry me between them. We walked through forest, then fields, and eventually we managed to find a cobbled path.

'By nightfall, we were so exhausted that we flung ourselves on the ground by the side of the path and we fell asleep almost straightaway.

'When a *clip-clop* sound cut through my sleep, I wasn't sure whether it was real or if it had been created by my tired brain, like those travellers who dream up an oasis in the dry desert. But then I heard a horse somewhere close, and I opened my eyes to see an old woman walking towards us. I say old, but I'm sure she was much, much younger than I am now. Age seems so different depending on how old you are, doesn't it? She was probably not much older than fifty. I thought of her as our saviour.

'She got the boys to help her lift me on to the back of her cart and then she sat us down among her milk crates and covered us with a huge canvas sheet. We were so relieved that we had found someone to look after us that we just sat there holding hands like little children. I told myself that everything would be fine now.'

I could tell by Ania's expression that things didn't turn out fine, and I gripped her hand, scared of what she would say next.

'We'd been travelling for a few minutes when we heard shouting,' she continued.

'"Stop! Get down!" It was a man's voice with a heavy accent. I didn't even have to peep out from under the sheet to know that it was an enemy soldier. The only thing we didn't know was whether he was alone, or whether there was a whole army there.

'We heard the sound of our woman getting down.

'"Where are you going?" the horrible voice demanded.

'"Home. It's not far from here – just round the left turn." I was surprised at how calm she sounded.

'"And where did you come from?"

'"The market. I was selling my milk."

'"Your milk. She was selling her milk," the voice repeated mockingly. There was the sound of stifled laughter. So there was more than one of them.

'"Show us," the voice demanded suddenly and the breath caught in my throat. "Sommer, check the woman is not a dirty liar." That was it. I was certain then that we would die, and I imagined that before we did, we would be tortured for trying to escape.

'I held my breath and clutched Henryk's hand, and then the canvas sheet was lifted from above our heads and a face peered in.

'It was a face that I remember in such great detail that I can paint every hair and wrinkle on it. He wasn't what most people would think of as a beautiful man. He was middle-aged, with mousy-brown hair, a thick beard and a scar on his left cheek in the shape of a question mark. But his gaze was deep and kind, and I could see how shocked he was when he saw me. I think he almost didn't notice the boys – he looked at me, and my ankle, which was very swollen by then, and I could have been imagining it, but I thought that his head shook slightly. Then he raised his finger to his lips.

'"Well, anything interesting?" yelled the horrible voice.

'I stared back at the man and thought that it was the last time that I would be free. The silent seconds stretched out between us like a thread that would snap at any moment.

'And then, to my shock, he said in a calm voice, "No. Nothing. Milk crates."'

'He let you go?' I asked Ania. I couldn't believe it. 'But why?'

'I asked myself that question for many days afterwards. I stared at his face as it broke into a smile. It was a sad smile, but for a moment, it brought together two people on opposite sides of a great divide, and it felt wonderful. It felt really wonderful.

'"You must be careful," barked the horrible voice to our woman, "a *fraulein* like you shouldn't be out on her own." He laughed again and there was a sudden smacking sound, skin on skin. He must have hit her. I could feel Adam's body tense when he heard it, and it looked like he was about to get out and attack the man. We managed to pull him back, and I could barely believe it when the *clip-clop* of the horse's hooves could be heard. We were on our way again.'

Ania paused and I waited with my eyes closed for her to continue. In my mind, I was still there with her on that cart, underneath the old sheet, staring at Sommer hopefully. I didn't want the moment to end.

'I think that's all for today,' Ania said quietly, and when I looked up, I saw that she was rubbing each of her shoulders with the opposite hand, as if she wanted to warm herself. I helped her to her feet and picked up the parrot walking stick. Then I led her indoors and sat her down in her favourite chair in the conservatory.

'So that's why you call him "The Good Solider"?' I asked her. 'Even though he was part of the enemy army who did awful things?'

Ania smiled eagerly, and I knew that I'd hit the nail on the head.

'Yes, because actually it's not about sides, when you think about it, is it? He did what he could to be good and kind in the circumstances that he was in. The world around us was filled with darkness, but within him there was more light than dark. That is all that matters. That's all that you can ask of any human being.'

TWELVE

I couldn't sleep that night. I wasn't sure why Sommer had decided to spare Ania but I knew it was incredibly brave of him to risk that for something he believed in.

And the more I thought about this, the more I realised that I would never be remembered as brave or good. If anything, it would be the opposite. When I shut my eyes, a rolled-up letter appeared before me, tucked carefully behind the glass of a museum cabinet. A dense crowd was gathered around, people pushing past one another to read the sign that explained what it was.

Those who managed to draw closer recoiled in disgust. It took me hours to get to the front of the queue, and when I did, I saw the familiar crest along with Mr Kim's scanned signature, and I knew. I read the title of the exhibit: *Letter from a Bully to an Innocent Boy.*

The words were still circling in my head as I went downstairs to breakfast. I felt dizzy with tiredness.

'Are you feeling OK, love?' Mum asked. I must have looked terrible for her to notice.

'Fine,' I mumbled. I didn't want to get into it. I knew that there was nothing that they could do to help.

The doorbell went as we were finishing eating and Dad answered it.

'Hello, Gemma,' I heard him say. 'What brings you here so early?'

'I thought I'd walk the long way round and pick Kat up on the way to school,' she announced, coming into the kitchen.

'Would you like a croissant?' Mum asked. Why was it that even she couldn't see through Gem and realise how mean and unkind she could be?

'I'm all right, thanks. I've already had breakfast.' She was bursting to speak to me. Her hair wasn't as perfect as usual and she had a sheen of sweat on her forehead. I imagined that she must have run all the way to our house.

I took a deliberately long time gathering my stuff so that I could delay the conversation we were about to have. I probably managed about three minutes.

'Did you get it?' she asked as soon as we were out of the door. 'I saw you talking to him outside school yesterday. Nice work. Did you get his number?'

'Yes.'

'Great. You're a star,' she said, looking at me with genuine admiration as we got on the bus. 'How did you manage it?'

I lowered my voice and looked frantically up and down the bus to make sure that there was nobody there who we knew. I spied a couple of girls at the back from our class, but they seemed far enough away to be out of earshot.

'He just gave it to me. He said his mum's been encouraging him to invite some of his new friends round.'

'Wow, he's deluded, isn't he? Anyway, you've got it. That's the main thing. I've been thinking about what to send him. I reckon we'll start off with something small. We'll say, *Hey, I've been thinking about you a lot. You're awesome. Thanks for giving me your number xxx.*'

'What? Why?' I asked her. 'Don't you just want to tell him where to turn up and what time?'

'It's all about making him believe that you're properly into him,' she explained, as if it was the most obvious thing in the world. 'We'll send that this morning and then we'll build it up from there. The next message can say: *I thought there was something magical about you from the first time I saw you.* Trust me – I know how to handle these things.'

'But that's mad. He'll know that I don't mean it. Nobody says stuff like that.'

'He's not just anybody. He's the world's biggest freak. It's exactly the sort of thing he'll believe. He believed the charity-day thing, didn't he?'

'That was different. And what if he tries to talk to me?'

'Ah, yeah, that's the thing. You're going to have to avoid him until we get him to agree to the meeting. Pretend you fancy him, but you're shy. I'll be with you all the time so you don't have to worry. I'll make sure that I lead you away when I see him coming.'

'But why do we have to do all this?' I didn't intend for the question to sound so much like a wail.

'What do you mean, Katherine?' she snapped.

When she used my full name, I knew that I was in trouble. She looked at me and I was surprised her voice shook a bit.

'How can you even ask that? He waltzed in trying to show everyone that he was the best and the cleverest, wanting to imply I'm the idiot. And then he stole my limelight in the one thing that I love the most.' It was the first time she'd admitted aloud how much that had got to her, and I could see by the way she suddenly clamped her hand over her mouth that she hadn't meant to say it.

'He can't get away with everything he's doing,' she said hurriedly. 'Someone needs to put him in his place and it should be us – that's why we're doing Operation Loser Boy. Don't you want to help stand up for me? Because, you know, you don't have to. I can get Ruby or Dilly…'

'Well, maybe you *should* get one of them to do it instead. I don't want to be messaging him stuff that isn't true! He probably wouldn't believe it anyway, but if he does, it will be so cruel.'

It was the first time that I'd said something like that to Gem. I felt strangely lightheaded.

She was shocked, and then the shock turned into her getting really, really mad.

We didn't look at each other for the rest of the bus journey, or the short walk into school.

It was only when we sat down at our desks that she said, 'Give me your phone!'

'No,' I replied firmly. But she snatched it out of my hand before I could stop her. She found his name in the list of contacts and started typing.

I tried to grab it back, but she was too quick. And that was when I couldn't bear it any longer. Rage pounded through me. This was it. I would tell Julius the truth at the next possible opportunity. I no longer cared what Gem thought, or how mad she'd get.

Julius turned in his seat almost as soon as Gem hit 'Send' and I ducked under the desk pretending to look for something in my bag. Telling him would be much harder than I imagined.

The whole morning, I felt as if I was walking on burning lava, just like Girl 38. In fact, the only way I managed to get through the day was by pretending to be her. I tiptoed around, trying to dodge the Vilk as he sneaked from one classroom to another. The trouble was that he was swift of foot and appeared in places where Girl 38 least expected him.

The main thing was to keep your head down and be constantly on the look-out for his mane, which was a particularly bright, pale yellow. Whenever Girl 38 saw it, she was careful to step behind the trunk of a moon tree to avoid being caught.

Gem still wouldn't give me my phone back and sent another message to Julius before lunch. After that I decided that it was safest to hang out in the quietest and most hidden corner of the library until the final period of double maths. I knew it was very unlikely that he would find me there and I sat doing my homework with a stash of books in front of my face.

But when I got back to our form room, she was busy with my phone.

'What are you writing now?' I whispered frantically.

'Something very important.'

She looked at the message, satisfied, and hit 'Send'. 'I was just reassuring our friend Julius, who says: *Thanks for the compliments. Do you mean them, or are you joking? Want to meet me on the way out of school? J.* So I've told him, *I think you're so hot, but I'm too shy to talk to you. The way you look at me makes me shiver.*'

'What? What does that even mean?' I asked Gem. '"Makes me shiver" – nobody says that kind of thing.'

She sighed. 'Yes, they do, Kat,' she said, giving me a pitying look. 'Come to mine tomorrow around midday. Dil and Ruby are coming. Mum will make us pancakes and then we can plan our strategy. Oh, and you can have your phone back then – maybe.'

I forced myself to keep my lips zipped, because I knew that if I didn't, something terrible (which I might regret) would come out. I breathed slowly in and out three times, counting the length of my breath in my head. *One caterpillar. Two caterpillars. Three caterpillars.*

It sounds silly now, but Mum taught me to do it when I was little. I used to get frightened in some situations and my heart would start racing. I was scared of big dogs, and one time, a huge Alsatian came running up to me in the playground. I lay on the ground and shut my eyes, and I remember that there was a moment when I couldn't even breathe.

Finally, Mum reached me, put me on her lap and rocked me. The dog had gone back to the other side of the playground. From a distance, I could tell it wasn't dangerous, but in that moment the feeling was so overwhelming that I couldn't focus on anything. Not even getting the air in and out of my lungs. The memory made me think of Julius and his sheep.

Ever since the dog incident, whenever I'm scared, or angry, or sad, I always use the breathing strategy. I hadn't had to use it for a long time. When my heart went back to feeling normal, I tried to cheer myself up with the thought that there was only one double period left and then, after school, I could visit Ania. I started to count down the minutes.

She was there in the conservatory when I got home and I could feel my shoulders slumping with relief as I caught a glimpse of her from my bedroom window. I ran straight over to see her. Her long grey hair was piled on her head and held up with something that I thought was a large pencil, but turned out to be a knitting needle.

She'd finished the charcoal outline of Sommer and I could see that she was adding colour, but slowly – building up from the palest peach of the skin to a darker pink hue around the cheeks. The eyes she'd coloured a deep-sea green.

I sat on the armrest of her chair to watch her work.

'I've had the most terrible day,' I said.

'I can see.'

She went to the kitchen and re-emerged minutes later with a cracked spotty teapot and the usual two mugs with slices of lemon and a spoon of honey already inside. She handed me the Victorian tea glass.

'Maybe today you want to tell me something about it?' she asked quietly, and when I looked into her eyes, it struck me that she was the only person who sensed the storm hidden in me – she had seen it all along and was patiently waiting for me to confide in her when the moment was right, and it finally *was* right. I knew that I could trust her.

'I'm part of something that I didn't want to do – a cruel thing that I know is going to badly hurt another person. I'm...'

Tears were filling my eyes. Any second now they would brim over.

She sat next to me and closed her bony hands gently around mine. They were warm.

'And has it already hurt this other person?'

'Sort of, but I think it's about to get a whole lot worse.'

'Sometimes when difficult situations like this happen, it is good to park them for a moment, if you can. Your mind needs a break from worrying, and then when you go back to thinking about them, you might surprise yourself with a solution. Perhaps I could help?'

'How?'

'Well, I wondered if you still want to hear the rest of my story? I think you might find it interesting, maybe even a bit useful in the circumstances.'

I was amazed at how she always knew the right thing to say.

'Definitely. It's what I came for.'

She put down her paintbrush, covered Sommer with a clear plastic sheet, and moved round the table to sit opposite me. Then she smiled at me and her eyes creased up at the corners like they always did.

THIRTEEN

'The woman who had rescued us in her milk cart was called Ela. She ran a small farm with her son on the outskirts of the city. She was strict and reminded me of my headmistress at school, but I could tell straightaway she had a good heart. What I liked about her was that she was very organised, and at that point we needed somebody to tell us what to do.

'She looked after us well and made sure I properly rested my ankle before helping the boys with gathering the corn. I was naïve because I imagined we would stay for a week, maybe two weeks, and then we'd be able to go back home to our families. But Ela's friends and neighbours brought us news from the wider world that enemy soldiers were still in the area, and we'd be caught for sure. It had been early September when we boarded the train and now suddenly there was snow on the ground outside and Christmas was coming.'

'You weren't with your family for Christmas?' I couldn't imagine spending Christmas anywhere other than home.

'No. I missed them desperately, and I couldn't stop thinking about what they were doing. Who had taken over my usual job of decorating the tree with candles? Had my grandparents come over to visit? Did my family have enough to eat? There were rumours about food shortages everywhere. I wanted to send word to them that I was all right, but Ela advised me against it. She said that post was being intercepted and told me that I could put my family in danger if the soldiers knew I had escaped.

'There wasn't a day that went by when I didn't think of Mila too. As I closed my eyes in bed at night, I would often see her. Sometimes she was sitting at the big old oak table in our kitchen where we used to do our homework together. I tried to believe that she had managed to get home and she was waiting for me to come back to her. But, on bad days, when I was feeling very, very sad or lonely, I saw her sitting in a dark room packed with other people, all shivering from cold, hunger and illness.

'Ela bought me an exercise book. She thought I might want to write a diary to help fill my time while they were all working and I was resting. I knew straightaway that I would use it to draw my first portrait of Mila.'

'You left, didn't you?' I guessed. 'But not to go home. You left to find Mila.'

'Yes,' Ania said, looking at me, surprised. I was secretly pleased that I'd managed to get it right.

'There was a night in early January when I had a dream. Mila was calling to me from across the fields, sending a Morse-Code signal which repeated the word "help" over and over. The light flickered through the dark and I ran towards it, but the closer I got, the fainter it became. Suddenly, I thought I could see her and my hand reached to touch hers, but then… my fingers gripped nothing but air.

'Something broke in me the following morning,

and I decided I couldn't wait any longer. I needed to act.'

'But how did you know what to do?'

'Ah, I have always been a very good listener. I listened to the conversations of Ela's clients who visited every day. I found out everything that went on in the outside world. Adam hadn't been lying about the village created within the awful walls. The local shopkeeper, Mr Pasek, seemed to know the most about it. Like me, he had a Jewish friend who had been captured and sent there.

'"The village is basically four streets," he said. "The entrance is so narrow that only a single car can pass by. All the buildings within have been taken over by the devil's army. There are food deliveries once a day but it's barely enough to feed a quarter of the people."

'I could tell he wanted to do something to rescue his friend, but his fear was stopping him, and speaking to Ela was the only way he could make himself feel a little better.

'Every time I got a new piece of information, I wrote down what I knew about the "devil's village", because that's how I had started to think of it in my head.

'The things I'd managed to find out were:

1. It was in the city, about two days' walk from where we were, going north.
2. It was right in the centre of town, with the entrance near the old post office.
3. This entrance was patrolled twenty-four hours a day by soldiers stationed outside.
4. The walls were incredibly high, made of concrete slabs and topped with barbed wire.
5. There were rumours that some brave people had managed to smuggle food in by throwing it over the lowest parts of the wall.
6. I hadn't heard of anyone successfully escaping.

'I decided to tell Adam and Henryk about my plan. When I look back now, I think I wanted them to say I was mad and the whole idea would never work. That way, I could carry on living like Mr Pasek, telling myself I would help, if only it were possible. But it turned out the boys had a plan of their own.

'"We've been meaning to tell you for a few days," Adam said, looking at the ground. "Only we were worried about how you would take the news. We're leaving at the end of the week to join the army. We can't sit around here waiting for something to happen to us. We're going to fight. We're going to show them!"'

'So when they said that, it made up your mind?' I asked Ania. 'You had to go and be brave. There were no excuses.'

'Exactly. If they were going to risk everything and go into battle to save our country, then I would never forgive myself for not going into my own personal battle to save my friend.

'I decided that it would be easiest to leave in the early morning when the rest of the house was asleep. I wrote Ela a thank-you note and left her a portrait I'd drawn of her working in the kitchen. Then, I packed a few bread buns, a flask of milk and some apples into a cloth sack, put on two of the warmest jumpers she'd knitted for me, and opened the door into the falling snow. When I realised that it came up to my ankles I almost changed my mind, but I thought about Mila sleeping in far worse cold every night, and I forced my feet to continue stamping through the white blizzard. By the time I got on to the main road, my legs were soaked through up to my knees.

'Have you ever walked through a frightening area that you didn't know, alone?' Ania asked me.

I shook my head. I'd once lost Mum on the beach when we were on holiday and it took us about fifteen scary minutes to find each other, but I knew that wasn't the sort of thing that Ania meant.

'It was awful, my dear Katherine. Every noise on that ghostly road startled me. Every whine of a fox, even the rush of wind in the cornfields made me stop and flatten myself to the ground.

'I walked for hours and the worst part of it was I didn't even know if I was going in the right direction. My ankle began to hurt again, I'd eaten all the food I'd taken with me – my body needed it to keep going – and I was running out of water. I was suspicious of every cart that went by, and I didn't dare ask the drivers how far away I was from the town, because I was so scared of being taken straight to the soldiers.

'When it started to get dark, I was delirious from tiredness, so when I heard the low whirring sound somewhere in the distance, I ignored it and carried on walking. But it got louder and louder. I realised too late that it belonged to a motor car, and by the time its beams illuminated my back, there was no running or ducking to be done.'

My insides tightened. 'Were they enemy soldiers? Did they take you to the camps after all that?'

'It was two men from the enemy army. When they switched on their torches I could see the navy uniform. They spoke to each other in a language I didn't understand, and I knew that I was finished.

'"What are you doing?" the soldier asked. He did not sound as cruel as the moustache man outside the church, or even the milk-truck soldier who had bullied Ela, but my voice still caught in my throat.

'"Why are you walking at night on your own? I don't need to tell you that it is freezing and dangerous out here."

'I just stood there and I couldn't say a word, but he didn't give up on getting an answer from me. He walked closer and waited a short distance away, his torchlight focused on the lower part of my face so that it didn't blind me. Then I heard the footsteps of his colleague coming closer.

'"I'm looking for my friend," I eventually managed to say. "I know that she is in the city and I'm going to find her. I wanted to get some transport, but I couldn't, so I'm walking."

'None of it was technically a lie, but I avoided giving details because I still hoped that they might let me go if I didn't act suspiciously.

'"I see," said the soldier. I heard a note of disbelief in his voice. He sighed. "Sommer, this girl is searching for a friend."

'The name sparked a memory in my mind, and I studied the second man as he approached. His colleague turned the torch beam on to him and my heart leaped. It was the soldier who had let us go free when we were in the milk cart. I saw that he recognised me too.

'"I know. I heard what she said," Sommer answered, and, after a pause, he suggested, "I think we should take her to the city."

'I had no way of guessing what he was planning,

but, strangely, his colleague agreed with him. He opened the door and motioned for me to get into the back of the car.

'For a second I thought about running, but it was madness. I wouldn't have got anywhere far on the icy ground, in the dark. So I gave in – I had to. I stepped into the back of his car.'

+ . · . + ✦
· . · .
✦ ·

I was still imagining Ania trudging through the snow as I sat in my bedroom later that evening working on the comic.

I stared at Girl 38, who had just caught sight of the Vilk emerging from between two shadowy trees.

'What would you have done?' I asked her, but she looked as frightened as I was.

FOURTEEN

Next day, First Mate Hawk Eye had to stay on the ship with Captain Eagle Heart so she sent Girl 38 out on her own. But almost as soon as she set off, Girl 38 saw that the Vilk she'd been running from yesterday was still following her. This time, he was so close that she could look him straight in the eye, and when she did, she realised that he wasn't half as frightening as she had imagined. In fact, he was looking at her as if he wanted to be friends. She dared to allow him to move closer, and he gently brushed against her with his tail, encouraging her to follow him.

'How ya hanging?' asked Mum when she came into

the kitchen and saw me drawing. 'What are your plans today? Are you chilling with your bros?'

When I didn't laugh, she came over to give me a hug. 'Are you OK, darling?'

I nodded. I was far from OK, but I wasn't sure how I would even begin telling her what was wrong.

'Want to come into town with me? Dad's playing football this morning and I thought I would take advantage of the good weather and check out the new flower market that Rhonda at work's been going on about. Apparently they have loads of deals on bouquets. It might be good fun, and then we can go for lunch. What d'you think?'

I would have loved to spend the day with her doing exactly that, but it wasn't possible. I knew that Gem would hunt me down if I told her that I couldn't come to hers and, anyway, I wanted to get my phone back.

'I can't. I'm sorry. I have to go to Gem's.'

'You don't *have* to do anything,' said Dad, coming into the kitchen with his football kit. 'Tell her you can't go if you'd rather do something different. I would, if I were you.'

'No, it's OK. I want to go,' I said. I tried to sound cheerful, but even I could tell that it wasn't convincing.

They both threw me a sceptical look, but didn't say anything.

I decided that before I faced Gem and everything she had in store for me, I would spend some time with Ania. I hoped that being with her and hearing more of her story might help me with the rest of the day.

It was a wonderfully warm autumn morning and Ania had thrown her living-room windows wide open, as if to welcome in the sunshine. She was holding a croissant in her hand as she opened the door.

'Good morning,' she said, and I realised, pleased, that she wasn't surprised to see me. I was beginning to feel completely at home in her house. 'I was just having some breakfast.'

'I've already had mine, but shall I make us some tea?' I said. 'I want to hear what happened after you got into Sommer's car. Or do you have other plans for the next hour?'

'No plans, except sitting here by the window,' she said. 'What is the word that you use for enjoying the sun? Almost like a cat?'

'Lounging?'

'No it begins with "b" – "basking", that's it,' she announced. 'You go and put the kettle on, and then I will continue speaking as we bask.'

Moments later, we were seated in the conservatory, looking out on a space which was no longer the Jankowski Jungle. Then Ania closed her eyes, and I decided to shut mine too, so that I could see her world completely.

'Sommer's car had a leathery smell which reminded me of my father's horse saddles. In the front the two men continued their conversation in hushed voices. I had no idea what they were saying, but I was relieved they weren't angry. I was so exhausted that I didn't even realise when I fell asleep.'

'You fell asleep? How could you? What if they did something to you…?'

'I know, Katherine. I cannot explain it, but somehow I felt safe knowing that Sommer was there. I had started to see him as a good omen, or a guardian angel. I woke up to him calling out to me, worried. His colleague had gone.

'"I dropped the commander at his quarters en route. You were asleep," he said, when he saw me looking around the car. "Are you a bit warmer now? Can I ask – what is your name?"

'"Ania." I didn't see a reason to hide it from him. "Why are you helping me?" I asked him quietly.

'"Because when I saw you lying there, hiding among those milk barrels, you reminded me of my own daughter," he said. "The commander thinks I'm taking you to the labour camp in the north of the city. He thinks that you are fit to work in the fields."

'I nodded. I understood. This was the best that he could do for me. He needed to follow orders.

'"But where do *you* want me to take you?" he asked.

'"Oh, anywhere. As close to the city as possible," I said.'

'Were you scared that he might get mad at you?' I asked her. I could never imagine myself being so brave with an enemy soldier.

'Of course. But I had changed since I left home. Sometimes I did not recognise myself – I was desperate, and I think that made me bolder.

'Sommer insisted that I wasn't allowed to walk alone in the city at night and that I needed to give him an address to take me to. I told him that I only knew that the place was near the old post office. It took a couple of seconds for him to realise what I meant. When he did, his expression changed.

'"Are you saying your friend is inside the ghetto?"

'*Ghet-to*. The word tripped off his tongue like a rhyme. I'd heard it before, being spoken by Ela's neighbours, and by Adam and Henryk, but it was only from Sommer's lips that it sounded real.

'"Yes. I'm not sure, but I think so."

'"Why do you think so?"

'"She's from a Jewish family and she was snatched from outside our church…" I remembered the exercise book in my pocket. I opened it to the page with Mila's portrait and showed it to Sommer.

'"Mila Kaufmann." He read my scribble in pencil at the bottom. Then he rubbed his face with his hand

and balanced his elbows on the steering wheel. We sat in silence for a few moments, the cobbled street stretching ahead. There were dots of light from street lamps in the distance, but I could tell that the black sky was already lightening. Soon it would be morning and daylight would catch us.

'"Ania," he said eventually. "Forget about your friend. It might be that she was never there. Or it could be that she's no longer here."

'My fists tightened by my sides. "I can't. I promised her. I promised her I'd do everything I could to find her. And so far, I haven't done *every*thing."

'He sighed and looked me straight in the eye. It was a chilling look, as if he was trying to tell me something important without words.

'"I'm going to get out here. Thank you for everything," I said to him and I opened the door to leave. I was worried that he might suddenly change his mind and drive me straight to the labour camp.'

'But he didn't?'

'No. He told me he knew a place I could stay for the night. Before I could protest, he'd started the car again, and we were driving swiftly through empty streets. We stopped outside a bakery. Sommer ushered me out of the car and walked around the side of the building. Here there was a small door, almost invisible from the main street. He brought his finger to his lips, then he rapped on it three times and we waited.

'The man who opened it was old and bald. He was dressed in nothing but a pair of cloth trousers and battered boots, and his skin was brown and leathery. When he saw Sommer, he motioned for us both to come in. The sudden temperature change made my whole body shudder. I could see the huge ovens at the back of the room, and there was an overwhelming smell of fresh bread.

'"Sorry for coming unexpectedly, Roman," Sommer said.

'"All your visits are unexpected, but you are always welcome here. You know that. Can I get you something to eat?"

'And before we had a chance to answer, he was inviting us to sit at the table, and he brought a plate of bread rolls with a slab of butter.

'"This is Ania," Sommer said, when he observed the old man watching me with interest. "I hope that she might be able to stay here with you for a short while."

'If Roman was surprised, he didn't show it.

'"She's welcome to. But it's not very pleasant, I'm afraid. Terribly hot," he said, spreading his arms, "and the smoke gets in your chest. I can only offer you the loft. It's the furthest away from the ovens."

'It was a tiny room with sloping ceilings and a mattress on the floor. But it was all I needed – and, most of all, it was warm.

'I lay down and tried to listen in on the conversation of the men downstairs, but I could hear nothing but a low murmur…'

Ania's eyes were still closed as she said this and I knew she was back in that warm loft.

I left her there, still basking in the sunshine as I made my way with a heavy heart to face Gem.

FIFTEEN

The front door of Gem's house was open. I walked in to the sound of crying coming from the kitchen, somebody playing an out-of-tune piano, and a voice screaming, 'Tasha, get down here right now!'

It had been like this ever since I could remember. Gem was one of five kids, which meant that going into her house was always like walking into a hurricane. It was the exact opposite of everything I was used to at home – peace, quiet and tidiness. Gem's mum, Liz, always looked a bit tired, and I sometimes felt bad coming round because it seemed like I was only adding to her workload by being there.

'Hi!' I shouted as I walked in. The only way of being heard in Gem's house was to be louder than anyone else.

'Oh, hiya love,' said Liz, wiping her hand across her forehead. 'Gem and the girls are already upstairs. Here, this batch is for you all,' she said, handing me a plate of pancakes. 'Grab a tray and take it upstairs. Help yourself to the jam from the fridge, and the lemon and sugar are there on the side.'

I did as she said, and moments later, I was climbing the three flights of stairs to the loft conversion that Gem shared with her little brother, Stu. She ushered me in. 'Don't worry. The brat's out at his friend's place,' she announced. 'Come in.'

'Gem's got some news,' Dilly burst out before I'd even managed to sit down.

I was dreading what she was about to say, but it turned out that it wasn't what I expected at all.

'Arun's asked me out,' said Gem, turning bright red. 'He wants to go to the cinema next weekend. He's going with Jace and he said that I should bring a friend too, so I guess it's sort of a double date. I thought of taking you, Kat, but I decided to ask

Ruby to come with me. She's had a thing for Jace for a while anyway.'

Ruby started protesting, but I could tell she was chuffed.

'Great,' I said. 'That's exciting.' I crossed my fingers behind my back, hoping that the conversation would now be all about Arun instead of Julius, but no such luck.

'You're all going to have to help me choose my outfit,' said Gem. 'I've made a shortlist of five, and Dil says that I can try on the new dress that she got from her aunt in America. Anyway, today we're not talking about that. We need to form a plan of action for Operation Loser Boy. Speaking of which, this is his latest: *I got your message, but I don't think you mean it. Sounds like you're having a laugh at me.'*

'I've had a thought,' said Ruby, fiddling with her earrings and looking directly at Gem. 'I was watching a show on telly the other night in which people meet in a restaurant for their date and they get blindfolded before they walk in. Usually their blind date has brought them something. You know – like, a cake that they've made just for them, or a little present. I reckon that we should get Julius to do something like that.'

'How do you mean?'

'We get Kat to message him saying that he has to come at lunchtime to a special place that we've agreed, wearing a blindfold and holding a rose. It's because she's got a surprise in store for him.'

'Perfect,' said Gem, grinning, 'And then we invite everyone to come along quietly and watch him. You're an absolute genius!'

I could just imagine it. Julius standing in the middle of the stage in the school hall with a blindfold on holding a single rose, and the whole class staring at him, laughing.

'I think what we'll do,' Gem continued, 'is to spread the word by email. We each know the email addresses of at least ten people in the class, and we'll ask them to pass it on to others. We won't tell them what's going on – we'll just say that there's a secret event happening in the school hall at 1.45 p.m. on Wednesday and that they should be there because it will be super funny.'

'What if somebody tells Julius?' Dilly asked.

'Nobody will. He's not been here long enough. People wouldn't have his email address, and, besides, haven't you seen that he doesn't have any friends?'

'But… what do you want me to do when he turns up, thinking that I'll be there?' I asked. My voice sounded echoey, as if I was standing in a tunnel.

'Ah, you *will* be there, though, won't you? You'll be in the crowd, laughing at him! Maybe we'll even get him to say a few magic words before the surprise is revealed to him. That would be properly hilarious.'

'Yeah, that would be ace! Maybe something like, "I think you're a goddess. Let me see what you have planned for me…"'

They all chuckled. Gem was laughing so much that she toppled over, her elbow in the pancake plate.

My phone was lying on the floor, next to the cushion that I'd sat down on. Gem grabbed it and began to compose the message, her tongue sticking out in concentration. Dilly looked over her shoulder, grinning as she read.

I tried to protest, but no sound came out of my mouth. I just sat there, staring at them dumbly.

Gem read out what she was typing.

'*I thought maybe we could meet? I have a little surprise for you and I've been dying to show you. Meet on Wednesday on the stage of the school hall at 1.45 p.m.? Could you wear a blindfold to make it more exciting? xxx.*'

'What about telling him what he should say and to bring a rose?'

'Let's wait for him to agree to this. Kat will send that in her next message. We need to keep him interested,' said Gem. 'You can't tell him everything in one go. Trust me – I know how to work this.'

I tried my caterpillar trick to calm down, but I couldn't focus and kept losing count. I felt as though I was breathing through a straw and no matter how hard I tried and how wide I opened my mouth, I couldn't get enough air into my lungs.

And then I couldn't stand it any longer. I knew that I needed to get myself out of that room, otherwise something terrible might happen.

'Kat, are you OK? Do you not feel well?' asked Ruby. 'You look pale. Here, let me go and get you some water.'

'No. No, I'm sorry,' I muttered. 'I'm going to have to go,' I told them.

I picked up my jacket and ran down the stairs as fast as I could. It was only when I reached the end of the road that I stopped and leaned against the lamppost. The cold air flooded my lungs and my shoulders heaved. My heart thumped out the steady, reassuring message, *I'm OK. I'm OK. I'm OK.*

SIXTEEN

I stared back down the street to see whether they'd followed me, but there was no sign of anyone.

I pulled my jacket on. I still didn't have my phone. For a moment, I considered going back, but I knew I couldn't face it. I'd have to demand it from Gem at school on Monday. Whatever messages she sent with it couldn't cause more damage than she already had.

I walked home slowly. On every street I set myself a different challenge. On the first, I could walk only on the pavement slabs, on the second, only on the cracks, on the third, I had to reach each lamppost in less than seven steps. That way, I didn't have to think about Gem or Julius, or the messages.

I could focus on walking – on getting from one place to another. Everything else could wait.

Nobody was home when I got back as it was Lena's day off. Dad always went for a couple of drinks after football and Mum was probably still at the flower market. I found Chester in my room, lounging around in the middle of the bed, which probably meant that Ania wasn't at home either. Chester loved being sociable and only wandered off on his own when there was nobody around.

Through the window I could see Ania's easel and pots of charcoal on the back porch, so she probably hadn't gone anywhere far. Maybe she'd just popped out to the shops. I made myself a sandwich, because I hadn't eaten any pancakes at Gem's, and I sat out at the front waiting for her return.

Ania's front garden was almost worse than the jungle had been, if that was possible, but the amazing thing was that, despite the weeds, I could tell that it had once been beautiful. Deep orange chrysanthemums stuck out from between the dense grass, the pink heads of dahlias were visible by the front door, and the fence was lined with molehills that had grown over with grass, so that they resembled Hobbit homes. They reminded me of *Lord of the Rings* and then of Julius, and suddenly, unexpectedly, the tears that I'd been holding back for so long began to stream down my face. I thrust my balled fists against my eyes, trying to stop them in the same way that I used to at nursery when Gem called me a cry baby, and then I sat there, my head hidden in my knees, still clutching my soggy cheese sandwich.

A small, soft hand touched my shoulder.

'It's going to be all right, you know. Things never stay bad for too long. Everything changes. That is the only certainty. And that is what's so wonderful about this world,' said Ania's whispery voice, and then she put her arm around me. I let the sandwich drop and hugged her tightly.

'I'm not who you think I am,' I told her. 'I'm a bad person,' I sobbed into her beautiful silk blouse.

She didn't tell me off. Instead, she pulled me closer.

'I can't say that I know everything about you, Katherine. I haven't had the pleasure of getting to know you fully yet, but I can already say for certain that you aren't a bad person.'

'You don't know that. I've done some things that I'm not proud of.'

Ania laughed, and I glanced up.

'I'm only laughing because I cannot count the amount of times that I've said the very same thing to myself. I have *often* done things that I am not proud of.'

'You?'

'Absolutely. And I'll tell you a secret – bad people rarely regret what they've done, which means that if you do, you aren't a bad person.'

Now I spotted the portrait of Sommer. Ania must have propped it against the edge of the porch steps as she sat next to me.

'This man knows it more than most people,' she said. 'I had to take him to the art shop, as there was a tiny tear in the canvas, there in the top right-hand corner. They managed to fix it, fortunately.'

'That's good.'

'Come in with me,' she said. 'Or, if you want, you can wait here where you have the sun on your face.

You've dropped your lunch, so I'll make you a new sandwich with Polish ham. It will be wonderful, I tell you. I can almost taste it already.'

'Thank you,' I said, wiping my face.

'Will you tell me what he did next?' I asked, indicating Sommer's portrait. 'Did he come to check up on you at the bakery?'

'He did. I'll tell you everything. But first, I'll bring lunch and you bring two chairs from the kitchen.'

We sat, looking out on to the road. The ham was delicious, and my appetite was back instantly.

'So I've told you everything up to the part when I fell asleep in the loft. It was so warm up there, and the smell of baked bread was comforting. This bread,' she said, indicating her sandwich, 'is nothing in comparison. I must have slept for hours, because when I woke up, I could see that the light outside the window looked hazy. When I eventually came downstairs, I found Roman scrubbing the kitchen floor. I set to work helping him straightaway, even though he protested, and within a few hours we had cleaned the whole place. We talked as we worked and I asked him how he'd met Sommer.

159

'"He came to me one evening," he said. "Just as he did last night with you. I was frightened when I saw the uniform. I thought he'd come to tell me that I would have to shut down the bakery. But it turned out that he wanted the opposite. He asked me whether there was any way in which I could increase my bread production if he provided me with more flour – he wanted me to keep the arrangement a secret. I agreed. You see, he bought the extra bread from me and took it to feed the poor souls behind the wall."

'I told you before that I already felt safe with Sommer, but hearing this made me even more certain that he was a good man.

'When I told Roman my story, he surprised me by saying, "You know, if Mila *is* there, he's the man to help you find her. He'll look her up on the lists," said Roman, and put his big palm over mine. "I bet he'll come back very soon and let you know if she's there."

'"But even if she is, how will we ever get her out?" I asked him.

'I knew about the height of the wall and the

swarms of soldiers by the entrance. They made the rescue seem completely impossible.'

'Couldn't Sommer do something? He knew the soldiers who worked in the walled village, didn't he?' I asked, frustrated. 'It couldn't have been that difficult for him to get Mila out.'

'But, Katherine, what about the commander? What about all the other soldiers? He couldn't just take Mila without anybody asking questions. Remember that everybody was suspicious in those days. If they saw that Sommer was doing anything to help a girl who belonged to the "enemy", he would be in trouble. Not just that, but Mila might be punished too. This is why what he had done so far for me was already very brave and very, very risky.'

'But there had to be a way!'

'Well, Roman had an idea. He revealed it when he was certain we were alone. "There's an old underground sewer system that opens into the street next to the church," he said. "The entrance at the other end is right in the centre of the ghetto. I found out about this because we had some drainage problems a few years ago. There was a blockage in the system and the whole street was flooded."

'"Are you saying that you could rescue somebody by taking them through the sewers?" I asked him. I shuddered to think about it.

'"It's the only possible route. There's no way of getting over the wall. Some have attempted it, but it ended in catastrophe. I've also heard of people trying to dig tunnels, but there are soldiers patrolling the perimeter night and day. In all honesty, I can't even be certain about the sewer system. It could also be patrolled, or worse – it could be blocked."

'I didn't allow myself to think any more about this, because I didn't even know if Mila was there. Waiting to hear news about her from Sommer, without being able to do anything, was one of the worst feelings in the world, Katherine.

'Every night for the next few days, I thought that he might come back, but he didn't. I had nightmares in which he turned up at the back door with a sad look on his face, and I wouldn't even have to ask him to know why.'

'Why wasn't he coming?'

Ania raised her hand at my question, to show that I had to be patient.

'We didn't know, but on the third night, I'd had enough of waiting and I crept out in the middle of the night. There was thick sleet, but I didn't let it stop me. I was on a mission to inspect the sewers. I needed to know whether Roman was right about this being a possible route. I realised how dangerous this trip was, as there was a real chance that there were soldiers on secret patrol of the entrance. I walked as quickly as I could, and avoided street lamps completely, scared that I would be seen.

'When I got to the square outside the church, it took me almost half an hour to find the round drain cover that Roman had mentioned – it was so well-hidden under the mounds of dirty snow. Then it took all my strength to lift it. There were iron steps beneath, which led into the sewers below.'

'But what if something had happened to you?' I said. 'What if you'd slipped and fallen in, or if a soldier had found you? Nobody knew where you were, did they?'

'You're completely right. It was the most risky

thing I had ever done, well – maybe except jumping from the train,' she said, smiling. 'Still, I forced myself to go down those steps. It was even colder there than in the street, and it was pitch black. As soon as my feet felt the ground, there was a gust of wind which seemed to blow right through me. This was a good sign because it showed that the system wasn't blocked. I had taken Roman's torch with me, but the light from it was very, very weak. I could see maybe two metres in front of my face. The place was wet through. Every time I breathed out, there was a loud, echoing whisper.

'I walked on, although I could no longer feel my toes and I had to put my bare hands on the walls of the tunnel to stop myself from slipping on the ice. It felt as though I was walking for days, but really it was probably no more than fifteen minutes before I saw light spilling out ahead – the second exit. That was when I heard voices. They were speaking in my language, and I couldn't hear all the words, but I somehow knew that they belonged to the people beyond the wall. That was enough for me. I breathed out. I was sure now that Roman had been right and that the route could work.'

'Amazing. Did you tell Roman?'

'No. I was too scared. But two nights after my journey into the sewer, I was closing the trapdoor to the loft when I heard the knock. I climbed back down and waited for Roman to answer. And, just as in my nightmare, Sommer came in and his face was filled with worry. I felt instantly sick. I wanted to push him back into the snow and shut the door. I remember wishing that he wouldn't open his mouth so that I would never hear those terrible words. But he *did* open it, and he didn't say what I expected him to say.

'"Ania, your friend is there. She's in the ghetto. She's... she's not well, I'm afraid. She's not well. She's got a severe case of typhus. She may not..."

'But I wouldn't let him finish. I suddenly flung my arms around his neck and I cried and cried from happiness. Mila was there and she was alive. That was all that mattered to me in that moment.'

I waited for Ania to continue, but it looked like she needed a rest from talking. I breathed in deeply and listened to the wonderful silence of the front garden, interrupted only by the occasional flutter of a bird's wings in a tree, and the hum of traffic in the distance.

I glanced over at Ania. She had her arms folded in her lap and was looking calmly into the street.

I sat cross-legged in front of the picture of Sommer and stared at it. Then I took off the plastic cover to have a closer look. It was almost finished. There was only a little bit of work left to be done on adding texture to the hair and beard. He was half in shadow, as if he was standing to the side of a street-lamp beam. His hat was firmly on his head, and his army uniform was buttoned up under his neck, making him seem incredibly serious, but then I looked at his eyes and couldn't help but smile, because it was as though he was smiling right back at me.

In the corner of the canvas, Ania had written, 'The Good Soldier'.

Her words came flooding back. *The world around us was filled with darkness, but within him there was more light than dark.*

I peered at him again, and suddenly I knew

exactly what I had to do. I was pretty certain that I remembered Julius's address – 7, Jupiter Close. It was near to the swimming pool, so I knew how to get there. It was a gamble, because I had no idea whether he would be home, but it was worth a try.

'I need to go and do something important,' I told Ania. 'I'll be back soon.'

SEVENTEEN

Within minutes, I was walking out through Ania's front gate. I took the bus that Gem and I would normally get to the pool if Mum or Dad weren't there to drive. I was there much quicker than I'd imagined.

It was a quiet street, filled with old houses. I had to walk up a set of stairs to get to the front door and when I saw the huge brass knocker, I began to doubt whether I'd remembered the address correctly.

There was nothing else for it – I would have to knock. I rapped the knocker three times and waited. Nothing happened. I stepped away, deflated. And then, suddenly, there was a cough and the door swung open. A tall lady with long, pale-blonde hair appeared in the doorway. She was wearing a bright red jumper and had a pair of tortoiseshell glasses perched on top of her head.

'Hi,' I said, and my voice was shaking. 'Is this Julius's house? Or do I have the wrong place?'

'It certainly is,' she said. 'I'm his mum. He's at the pool, but he should be back soon. Would you like to come in and wait for him?'

Julius's mum was smiling at me, motioning for me to come in. 'I'm sure he'd love to see you,' she said.

Before I could change my mind, I found myself stepping into the hall.

She led me into a lounge which reminded me a little of Ania's house. But if her house was like a library, this one was a junkyard. There were piles of books and magazines in every available space. Oddly, most of them weren't propped against the walls. They stood in half-toppling towers all over the room and I had to navigate my way around them, being extremely careful not to bump into anything. To the left of me, an old-fashioned telephone balanced on top of a tall stash of nature magazines. Next to it, a tower formed of TV guides supported a pretty pink vase with a single wooden flower in it. One step in the wrong direction would cause the whole thing to come crashing down.

'We haven't had a chance to tidy up properly yet. We moved in a couple of weeks ago, you see, and there's been so much to do. This place was my family home when I was your age, and now it is again. Julius's grandmother needs us here now that his grandfather has passed away. She's sleeping in the bedroom down the hallway, so we mustn't be too loud. As you can see, my parents managed to gather heaps of stuff. I don't even know where most of it came from, to be honest.'

'It looks like they loved collecting things.'

'You could say that. Julius is having a lot of fun discovering new things in here all the time. The other day he found a very old-looking shield with our family crest on it and he got excited. He loves anything historical. Anyway, we're going to sort through gradually. But here I am blabbering on, and I didn't introduce myself properly, did I? I'm Sally.'

'I'm Kat.'

'Ah, you're Kat!' Her eyes widened. 'Julius told me about you.'

'Really?' I felt the heat in my face, and my heart sped up.

'He said you were lovely. I'm glad that he likes your school. I was worried for a while, you know. It's so different from his school in Yell. I'm pleased he's got a friend like you.'

'Yes,' I said. I was certain that my face was pink.

She brought a plate of biscuits from the kitchen and some juice.

'Help yourself while you wait,' she said, sitting next to me. 'Hey, do you know if anything might have happened to him yesterday?'

'Sorry?'

'I wondered whether he got a bad grade or something. He didn't say that anything was wrong, 'course, it's not like him, but I could tell.'

'I'm not sure,' I lied, and then, keen to get the attention away from myself and talk about something cheerful, I asked, 'Are you pleased about him getting into the swimming championships?'

'Oh, yes. He was always so brilliant at it. Kit taught him to swim in the sea up in Scotland when he was four, and he's loved it ever since.'

We both heard the front door slam.

'In here!' Julius's mum shouted, walking over to the door.

Julius was standing in the doorway, holding a bunch of roses, his hair still wet and standing on end. I realised he couldn't see me hiding behind the magazine tower.

'Those are beautiful,' said Sally. 'Where did you get them?'

'There was a flower market on and they were selling loads of bunches for a pound. I thought you'd like them,' he said.

'Well, they're gorgeous, but you may want to give one or two to your friend, Julius.'

That's when he saw me. His expression was a mix of shock and annoyance. This had been a bad idea after all, a very bad idea.

I was about to think of an excuse to make myself scarce, when Sally said, 'I'm going to go to see if Grandma's OK. Do you want to show Kat round?'

I followed him upstairs, neither of us saying anything. The floorboards creaked beneath us, and I studied the walls lined with black and white photos. They were of people in action – soldiers marching, a couple on a swing laughing, children mid-run in a playground. I loved them. They were so much better at catching the emotion of the moment than the posed pictures that we had at home.

'In here,' said Julius, pushing open a door.

We went into a big room with a huge bay window and chandelier-like lamp hanging from the ceiling. The whole place was such a perfect mix of old and new. The four-poster bed with its carved wooden frame was covered in a *Lord of the Rings* duvet, the chandelier had a solar system hanging from it which looked like it was made from a tennis ball, golf ball and different sizes of marbles, and figurines of *Star Wars* characters lined the bookcase. Unlike downstairs, everything was immaculately tidy. Julius looked at me and his mouth twitched.

I sat down on the edge of the bed and stared at my feet. I could no longer bear to pretend that there was nothing wrong.

'So…?'

'I'm sorry,' I whispered, before I could change my mind again. 'I'm sorry for the messages.'

For ages he said nothing. He sat cross-legged on the floor and looked up at me. I couldn't meet his eyes.

'You know, when you sent the first one, I thought you meant it. I was stupid enough to actually believe that somebody liked me. It made me feel better when I was beginning to think that the whole class was treating me as a joke. But then when I got the second one, I realised that… that you thought I was a right idiot.'

'No. It's not like that – I didn't send them,' I said. I realised how unbelievable it sounded and saw Julius raise an eyebrow.

'I know that they came from my phone, but it was Gem who wrote them and sent them.' There. I had said it now and there was no turning back. 'That doesn't mean I'm not to blame. I went along with her plan. Well, some of it.'

'What plan?'

I told him exactly what the gang had in store

for him and explained that it was us who'd put the maggots in his bag and arranged the whole dressing-up day thing.

'You did that? I thought it was the lads – a sort of joke initiation.'

So I was wrong. That day, he hadn't been looking at me because he suspected that I was to blame for what happened. He was probably hoping that I might be his friend and trying to suss out whether I felt the same.

'No, I think most of the boys in our class are pretty decent.'

'Unlike you?'

The question was like a punch in the stomach, but he was right.

'Unlike me,' I agreed.

We sat in silence as I had no idea what to say.

'Why did you come here?' Julius asked suddenly.

I stared at him. Wasn't it obvious?

'Because what we're doing is terrible,' I said. 'Because I don't want to be part of it any more. I didn't want to be part of it from the moment that we started, but I couldn't stop myself getting involved.

I've known Gem since we were three, and she's always been the one who's decided what we do. If I ever wanted to do something different, she would get mad and I was scared of her. I wanted to tell you the truth for weeks, but I was too much of a coward.'

As I spoke, his eyebrows disappeared higher and higher under his blond fringe.

'I liked you. I still do,' he said. 'I thought you were somebody who could be a mate.'

'I like you too.' I imagined it would sound weird saying it aloud, but it didn't.

'What made you suddenly decide to tell me? Why today?'

'It's not what, but who. A man called Sommer. And a woman called Ania. I'm actually not sure whether that's his first name or his surname, but I'm planning to find out more about him.'

Julius grinned.

'Can I meet him? This Sommer? And Ania?'

'Not Sommer... I wish you could, but it's a bit of a strange situation. He isn't around any more – at least, I don't think he is. But I can introduce you to

Ania who knew him very well. I think you'd like her a lot. But there's still much more I need to tell you before you meet her.'

'I don't have major plans,' he said casually.

I got up to leave, when a message pinged on his phone. He read it out to me:

'I can't wait to hear your reply. Will you meet me on Wednesday? Please don't keep me waiting too long xxx.

What should I respond? I reckon I'll just ignore it.'

I don't know what got into me, but I suddenly felt bold. Gem would already be furious when she found out what I'd done, so if I went a step further, it would make no difference.

'I think we need to play her at her own game. Do you mind if I reply for you?'

He passed me his phone.

'I'll be there. I'm looking forward to it. Is there anything I should bring? Xxx.'

As expected, a few minutes later we got another message.

'Bring a rose and sing me your favourite song

when you arrive. Don't forget to wear the blindfold. Otherwise it will spoil the surprise xxx.'

'You want me to go?' Julius asked after reading the messages.

'I want them to *think* that you'll go. Then we'll leave her a little surprise of her own.'

EIGHTEEN

Julius spent Sunday afternoon at mine as I told him Ania's story. Mum offered him her homemade chocolate brownies, and I could tell that Dad immediately warmed to him, because he kept asking him about Yell.

Julius sat on my bed with Chester on his lap, listening to the story so intently that at times I thought he'd stopped breathing. He'd rung his mum twice to ask if he could stay for longer. It was almost eight o'clock when I got to the part about Sommer coming to the bakery to tell Ania the amazing news about Mila, and he sat there, waiting for me to continue.

'That's it,' I told him. 'That's how much I know.'

'No way. You didn't find out if they rescued her?'

'Not yet.'

'Well, when can we hear the rest?'

'Let's try Tuesday. Why don't you come home with me after school and we'll see if we can go next door?'

I thought it would give me a chance to see Ania tomorrow myself and ask her whether it would be all right for me to bring Julius, and then I got nervous about whether I'd done the right thing by sharing her story with him without asking permission.

But my worries disappeared when I saw her.

'I would love to meet Julius,' she said. 'Make sure you bring him over tomorrow.'

Next day, we left school separately so that Gem didn't get suspicious. I had my phone back and she hadn't said anything about Saturday. We didn't want to give the game away before the big 'date'. Besides, Julius wanted to go via the flower shop on the way home. He met me outside my house just after four o'clock with a bunch of beautiful orange chrysanthemums for Ania, to match the ones in her garden. I saw that he'd straightened his tie and brushed down his blazer, as if preparing for a meeting with a VIP.

Ania opened the door to us wearing her peacock skirt and a stylish pink top that matched her lipstick.

'This is Julius,' I told her, although she already knew that. 'Julius, meet Ania. Julius was very interested in your story, especially in Sommer, and I wanted to show him your painting.'

'Welcome, Julius. If you are Katherine's friend, I'm sure you must be a wonderful person. Please come in.'

She took us both into the conservatory, where she'd already set the table with cakes and little sandwiches, like the high tea that you see people having in films. Sommer's finished portrait stood on the easel in front of the window.

'I have had nobody to talk to for so long and now it turns out that I have not one, but two fantastic young people,' said Ania. She looked at Sommer and said, 'You never stop bringing me good luck, do you?'

'These are for you,' said Julius, suddenly remembering the chrysanthemums. 'Kat told me that you have the same ones in your garden at the front.'

Ania's cheeks flushed. 'I do have them, but I've

let them run wild. You can hardly see them now, which is a shame, but these are wonderful.'

She put them in a vase and came to sit with us.

'Please tell me a bit about yourself, young man.'

'I'm in Kat's class,' Julius said. I could tell straightaway that he liked Ania. 'I've moved from Scotland so this is all a bit new, but I'm getting used to it. Kat told me your story – as far as you'd got up to. Will you tell us what happened next?'

'Of course,' said Ania. 'I think I remember where I got to. I'd just found out that Mila was alive, hadn't I?'

'Aye, Sommer came to tell you.'

Her face took on a look of complete peace. 'Yes, we were there in Roman's kitchen. I don't think that Sommer had had anyone hug him so tightly in a very long time, because he looked shocked. He sat at the table and looked at me hard. I realised that he was not at all excited.

'"If you want, I could get a message to Mila from you," he said to me. "But you should write it tonight, because soon it might be too late. I could find somebody to read it to her."

182

'"She can read. She did well at school. She was top…"

'"That's not what I mean, Ania," he said. "I'm sure she can read, but at the moment she's so weak that somebody would have to help."

'I could feel a cold dread at the base of my back. "I need to see her," I insisted. "I don't want to write anything if I could tell her myself."

'He sighed and put his head in his hands.

'"I was afraid you'd say this. That is why I debated for a long time today whether to tell you the truth. It's not possible, Ania. There is no way of getting her out, and even if there was, I'm afraid it's too late. She's much too sick. I don't need to tell you that typhus is a terrible illness and almost impossible to cure."

'I screamed at him. It was awful for me to behave like that after everything that he had done for me, but in that moment, rage engulfed me. Roman tried to hold me until I calmed down, but I fought him off.

'"I need to see her," I said to Sommer. "Please let me see her. I know of a way. I've even tested it."'

'Come on. You'd done so much to find her! He must have let you see her?' Julius burst out.

'Well, he was horrified when I told him I had been down in the sewers. He wouldn't stop reminding me that I could have slipped on my bad leg and ended up in trouble again, but deep down I could tell that he was impressed by how determined I was. He asked me the details of how I had found the sewer entrance, about the state of the tunnel and how far I had gone before I heard the voices from above ground. I knew he was fighting an internal battle.

'You might not believe it, but he eventually came around to my plan, and Roman immediately offered to go into the sewers himself, as Sommer would not let me step down there again. I was so touched by what they were doing that I couldn't stop crying. We planned the operation for the following night, as we realised how quickly we needed to act.'

'But what about the other entrance to the sewers? Weren't there always soldiers there? Wouldn't they see what Sommer was trying to do?' I asked, remembering the risks.

'It's a very good question, Katherine,' she said.

'There were always soldiers there, but they were managed by Sommer. He would organise it so for that one night, there would be no guard stationed in that area and would pass it off as an administrative mistake.

'The idea was that Sommer would bring Mila to a spot near the sewer entrance in the dead of night – if any of the soldiers spotted what was happening, he would say that he was taking her to the infirmary. Roman would travel through the sewers and carry her back to safety. The whole plan was a huge gamble, the chance of it working was tiny, and I knew I was putting both of their lives at risk. I could scarcely look at them, as I was so worried that they might change their minds.

'Roman had agreed with Sommer that he would be by the walled end of the sewer entrance at 3.30 a.m. the next night and he would only come up above ground when he heard the triple knock on the metal cover.

'I insisted that I should go with him to wait at the other end of the sewers. It was colder than ever that night and the tips of my fingers were numb within minutes. Just after three in the morning, Roman disappeared underground and I waited.'

'I bet you were scared out of your mind,' I said. 'Was it worse than jumping from the train?'

'Oh, a million times worse, because I was completely helpless and there was so much waiting. Each minute transformed itself into an hour. I got an awful sense of doom in the pit of my stomach and my mind came up with terrible scenarios in which they'd been caught. The panic rose in my throat and I was sick. And that was when I heard the sound. A clatter and heavy breathing coming from somewhere below my feet.'

'And what was it?' Julius asked, just as his phone rang. It was his mum, saying that it was late and she had to pick him up. He tried to argue with her about letting him stay longer, but she wouldn't let him.

'I'm afraid you're going to have to be patient,' said Ania, smiling mysteriously. 'We're almost at the "crux of the matter," as English people say.'

'She's amazing,' said Julius, when we walked outside to wait for his mum. 'D'you think they found Mila?'

'I'm not sure,' I told him honestly. 'I used to worry that she would never find her, but now that I've heard more of the story, I've started to hope.'

'It's a great thing – hope,' said Julius quietly, as his mum pulled up. 'I've recently started to hope a bit too.'

NINETEEN

Girl 38 walked behind the Vilk, still fearing that he was leading her to a trap. They went deeper and deeper into the forest until, finally, they reached a clearing. There, Girl 38 saw an amazing sight – there were stacks of food of every colour and shape. She saw mountains of juicy apples, much bigger than those on earth: tomatoes, carrots, bananas, figs, pineapples… the food stretched as far as the eye could see.

Just as she was taking it all in, she saw hundreds of Vilks emerge from behind the trees surrounding the enclosure. Had she been trapped? But, no… they huddled around her, pushing the best bits of food in her direction. They had gathered it especially for her. They wanted to be her friends.

'We're all set!' Gem whispered the minute she saw me in the classroom on Wednesday morning. 'Operation Loser Boy will be complete today.' She had that look on her face – the same one that she got before one of our teachers announced who'd won the creative writing prize or who had the highest score in our mock maths exam. She always knew that she would be the champion in the end.

'We've sent an email round to pretty much everyone in the class too, so they'll be there at 1.45 p.m. today. I can't wait. Make sure you tell me if he sends another message before lunch, yeah?'

I nodded. Gem had been very reluctant to give me back my phone on Monday, and constantly wanted to keep checking it for new messages. I allowed her. Julius knew how to respond to anything she sent.

At lunch, I could see how excited Ruby and Dilly were by the way that they were frantically scanning the room, trying to spot Julius. Gem looked as if she was about to burst. She nibbled on the edge of her crust of pizza and her fingers played a nervous rhythm on the table.

'I wonder what song he'll sing,' she said. 'I hope

it's something super embarrassing. Knowing him it will be.'

'Maybe the theme tune from *Lord of the Rings*,' Dilly guessed. 'Although it could be something totally weird that we've never heard, maybe something Scottish, like "Auld Lang Syne". You just don't know with him, do you?'

'I reckon it'll be something romantic from a musical,' said Ruby, closing her eyes. For a moment, it looked as though she wished she was the person being serenaded.

'Right, let's recap what's happening,' Gem said. 'Everyone's going to gather in the hall and we'll come in last. That way it will look as if we had nothing to do with it. If somehow Mr Kim or any other teachers hear about it and decide to come along, we don't want to be caught red-handed.'

'What if he hears everyone coming into the hall, freaks out and runs away?' asked Ruby.

'He won't, don't worry. I reckon he'll think that Kat's organised a little welcome party for him and invited our whole class.'

At 1.45 p.m. we were hiding out in the girls'

toilets near the hall. The plan had been to hold out until 1.50 p.m., but at 1.47 p.m., Gem lost her nerve and she pushed us into the corridor. There were murmurs coming from behind the hall doors, but no laughter.

'What's going on?' Gem wondered aloud. 'Maybe he hasn't started singing yet? He needs to get a move on.' I could see a flicker of doubt in her expression, but it was gone in an instant. We paused outside the doors. My heart was drumming. Eventually Ruby swung the doors open and we walked into the hall.

We joined the back of the crowd and I breathed out, relieved that Julius had managed to get everything right. Our excuse about wanting to 'practise the lighting for the school play' had worked and Mr Millicent had allowed Julius the keys to the lighting box where I knew he was watching from now.

The pink spotlight on the stage looked even more enchanting and mysterious than I'd imagined. Lying in the centre of it was a single rose and a small exercise book wrapped in paper. Of course, only I knew that's what they were, because they weren't quite visible to everyone from below.

'What is it?' someone in the front row asked. 'Is it the start of some sort of show?'

We waited for a few minutes and nothing happened. Eventually I heard Arun say, 'I'm going to go up there and check it out. I reckon it might be some kind of immersive theatre production. I've been to one of them before and you had to follow the clues. Whoever's planned this wants us to be part of the action.'

He pulled himself up on stage and picked up the two objects. He held the rose between his teeth, winked at the crowd, and then inspected the parcel carefully.

'Wow, it's addressed to Gem,' he said. 'Gem, are you here? Do you want to come and get it?'

Next to me, I felt Gem stiffen.

'What?' she asked. 'What's going on?'

'It's for you,' somebody in front of us told her. 'You should go up there.'

'It's… it's not for me.'

'It is,' Arun said, amused. 'Come up here and grab it, Gem. Or do you want me to open it for you? Maybe that's what we're supposed to do.' He lifted up his other hand, as if to tear the top of the wrapping paper when Gem suddenly wailed, 'No!'

She pushed through to the front of the crowd, got up on stage and ripped the parcel from his hand. Then she ran down the side stairs and disappeared through the double doors.

The crowd erupted into nervous chatter. I stifled the excited laughter that was bubbling up in my stomach. It had worked. Our plan had worked even better than we'd hoped. Next to me Dilly was nervously biting her fingernails.

'Oh, no! Oh, no! What are we going to do now? What was in the parcel?'

I shrugged my shoulders, but I knew, of course I knew, and what was more, I took full responsibility for it this time. I was no longer scared. I hadn't even bothered to disguise my handwriting. The parcel said simply, 'For Gem', and inside was *Girl 38,* which I'd scanned and copied especially for her.

It was mysterious enough for others not to know what it meant, because I didn't really want to humiliate Gem by letting everyone know what she'd done. I just wanted her to feel, for a moment, what it was like to be on the receiving end of one of her 'operations'. She would realise straight away that she was Hawk Eye.

Dilly and Ruby eventually decided that the right thing to do was to run after her, but I stayed back. The rest of our classmates soon got bored, accepted that it was some sort of joke that had gone wrong, and began to walk back to our form room. 'What was she trying to do?' I heard one of the boys mutter.

I hung back after everybody had left and then I ran up the stairs to the lighting box, where Julius was waiting for me.

'It went perfectly,' I told him. 'I hope it makes a difference.'

'If nothing else, it will get her thinking about who she's messing with,' he said, grinning. 'Hey, this box is grand, by the way. I reckon I might want to be a lighting technician. Look how many cool things you can do with these controls,' he said, swirling three different coloured lights round the stage to create a disco effect.

Gem didn't speak to me at form time or during double chemistry, which was our last lesson of the day. She made a point of switching seats with Ruby so that she didn't have to sit next to me. All three of them were ignoring me, which wasn't surprising. I knew that our friendship was over and, weirdly, I didn't mind. My heart was light and I felt better than I'd done in a very long time.

I saw Arun casting glances in Gem's direction, as if trying to figure out what she'd been playing at. I noticed that he still had our rose, which he'd picked up off the stage. He'd been goofing around with it in form period, twirling the stem between his fingers. I wondered if Gem had hoped that he might give it to her.

After school, I caught up with Julius at the gates and asked him if he wanted to come round. I thought that we might celebrate with some of Mum's chocolate brownies and then we could go next door. It was high time that we found out what happened to Mila.

TWENTY

'Are you sad that you moved down here? Do you miss Yell?' I asked Julius as we turned into my road.

'Aye, I mainly miss my dad and Kit. I try to talk to Dad on the phone every night and Kit's busy with uni, but he messages most days. I miss the sea – I always saw it on the way to school and I could tell exactly what mood it was in. When the waves were crashing like mad, I knew that it was furious, and when it was flat, like a cloud mirror, I could tell that it was thinking about what it would do next. I kind of miss the quiet sometimes too.'

'The quiet? How d'you mean?'

'Here, even in the middle of the night, when everything's switched off and I'm in bed, there's still noise. I can hear the hum of the traffic or people shouting in the street. In our old house, there would be complete silence, 'part from the wind against the windows.'

I shuddered. 'It sounds spooky.'

'Spooky? Nah. It was home,' he said. 'But I'm not sad I came here. It's an adventure. Everything's scary at first but my dad says that in frightening situations you gotta look for good people, so that's what I'm trying to do.'

It was strange, because it was exactly the sort of thing that I expected Ania to say to me.

The last few days had brought a cold spell, so Ania was no longer in her garden. Instead, when she led us into the living room, the fire was on and the smell of freshly-baked bread wafted in from the kitchen.

'I made it with you in mind,' she said. 'And I realise it's probably still too warm outside to have the fire on. But I had a feeling that you would come today and I wanted to create the atmosphere of the bakery. I thought that it could help you to imagine that you are there. Can I cut you a slice?'

'For sure,' said Julius. 'Smells amazing.'

We sat there with the flames dancing before our eyes, and although I could taste the delicious buttery bread in my mouth, and then the nuttiness of the brownies, I felt that I couldn't properly relax, as I was about to be told Mila's fate.

'You said you were about to reach the "crux of the matter". So what happened when you heard the noise beneath your feet?' I asked her nervously.

'Well,' she said, and I could see her grip the tissue that she was holding. 'When I heard the noise, I clambered down that ladder as quickly as I could and shone the torch ahead of me. At first I saw nothing but damp walls of earth, and I started to worry that I had imagined it. But then I saw Roman. My torch beam illuminated that wonderful old man who was carrying someone over his shoulder. It was someone who looked so much smaller, thinner and frailer than they should, but even from a distance of many metres I could tell that it was her.'

'It was Mila!' I jumped up and hugged Ania. Her withered cheek brushed my school shirt.

Julius shouted, 'You did it!'

'When I took Mila out of Roman's arms, I clung on to her as tightly as I could. In that moment, only the two of us existed, nothing else,' Ania whispered.

Then her voice faltered and she gazed down at her hands, opening her mouth as if she wanted to say more, but no words came out.

The silence hung between us, suspended on an invisible thread. I glanced at Julius and I could tell that, like me, he didn't want to snap it by speaking. Ania would carry on her story in her own time.

'For a long while I struggled to believe that the moment was real – that she was really there in my arms. She was so fragile – like a shadow of a person slipping through my fingers. Holding her close, I could feel the bones of her spine through the jumper that she had been wrapped in. It was navy and made of thick wool, and I was certain that it belonged to Sommer. Her breath came out in little gasps, and when she opened her eyes for a second, I wasn't sure whether she could actually see me.

'I whispered her name over and over and there was a moment when I thought that there might be a flicker of recognition, but it was gone almost instantly. We carried her back to the bakery and I was in a state of such shock that I didn't notice the dark figure lurking in front of our doorway until we were a few metres away.'

'Was it a soldier?'

'No, no. It was a young doctor, who had been sent by Sommer. I could tell he was extremely nervous and he did not want to be there, but I guess that he owed Sommer a favour.

'I laid Mila down on the couch at the back of the kitchen and got some water heated for the large tin bath that Roman used for washing. I cleaned her face, arms and legs. Her elbows jutted out in sharp corners and I could see the outline of her bones against her pale papery skin. Every few minutes a terrible cough tore through her body. I also saw an awful dark red rash spreading from her chest and stomach to her shoulders, as though she had been bitten all over by mosquitoes.

'The doctor examined her closely. He took her pulse, listened to her breathing and pulled back her eyelids gently.

'"A very severe case of typhus," he said eventually. "As I suspected, there's nothing I can do for her. The disease has progressed too far. If you're lucky, she may have a week left. The best that you can do is to keep her warm and comfortable and give her lots to drink. If you do, there is a possibility that she may become conscious enough to speak to you… before the end. You might have a chance to say goodbye."

'He said those last few sentences softly and apologetically, but I would not accept it,' said Ania, and she suddenly looked angrier than I'd ever seen her.

'Why? Didn't you think it was true?' Julius asked.

'No, I believed him about the typhus. But I also believed she could get better. Roman could tell how furious I was because he begged the doctor for some new medication that he had heard about – antibiotics. To start with, the doctor wouldn't give it to us, because he said he did not want to waste his small supply on such a "lost cause" but you can imagine how much I fought him.'

'And did he give in?'

'He had to. I wouldn't have let him leave

otherwise. For the next few days Mila mostly slept. As Roman still had to run the bakery, I looked after her myself. She only woke up for a few moments each time to take the medicine, drink lots of water, and have a tiny bit of porridge, which was all she could swallow. On the fourth day, when I was washing her face, her eyes focused on me properly for the first time and I thought I might be hallucinating when I heard her ask uncertainly, "Ania?"'

'She was going to be OK?' I whispered.

'Yes,' said Ania smiling at me. 'After she said my name, I knew for certain that she was going to be OK.'

TWENTY-ONE

'That didn't mean that Mila's recovery was easy from that moment – it was still very difficult and very slow. But Roman let us stay at the bakery for as long as we wanted to, and the medicine eventually started to work. It took about five weeks for her to eat some proper food, and another week for her to walk without my help. By then she was well enough to stay awake for a bit longer and she told us everything that had happened from the moment that I'd last seen her outside our village church.'

'Was it really terrible? Did she see people die?' I asked, scared of what I was about to hear. I'd started to build up an image in my head of life within the walled village – one of the darkest places in the world.

'Yes, many – some died of starvation; others of

disease. There was a little boy Mila made friends with who she desperately wanted to survive. She ended up giving him most of her own small allocation of food. Sadly, the typhus got him in the end. But Mila didn't see her efforts as a waste. She was glad that she had managed to help him and that he knew, before he died, that he was loved. That is the kind of unbelievable person she was.

'The soldiers had taken everything from her when she first arrived at the ghetto, but when she was waiting in line and realised what was happening, she managed to hide two small scraps of paper in her vest top. She kept them close to her heart and took them out to look at in the moments when she felt most frightened. One of them was a photograph of her mother – they were separated very early on – and the other was my sketch of us sending light signals to each other from our bedroom windows.

'She said to me: "I often looked through the grimy broken glass of the top-floor window of my room in the ghetto and hoped that there would be a Morse-Code light shining at me from the blackness."

'"Maybe there was," I said to her.

'"Maybe there was," Mila agreed.'

+ · · + •
+ · · ·
+ · ·

'What happened to her?' Julius asked nervously. 'Where is she now?'

We'd been listening for what seemed like hours. I wished he hadn't spoken because it broke the spell. In my head, I was still with the teenage Ania, standing next to Mila's bed, holding her hand and praying that she would continue to get stronger and stronger.

Ania was crying. There were big, round tears falling down her sunken cheeks, which she brushed away with a paint-spattered hand – but I saw that she was smiling at the same time.

'Mila, well – sadly she's no longer here. You have a good phrase for it in English – "passed away". I think it is a beautiful way to describe someone's soul, when it slips out of your grasp.'

'She died after all?' asked Julius, shocked. 'Despite you saving her?'

'Let me show you something,' said Ania and

she stood up, wobbling a bit on the parrot stick. I offered to help her, but she waved me away.

'Wait here. I will be back in a moment.'

When she returned, she was holding a framed photograph. I remembered seeing it earlier on one of the bookcases in her living room, but I'd never inspected it properly.

Julius and I peered at it closely. In the centre a young, newly-married couple were gazing into each other's eyes. The beautiful bride was wearing a fitted white dress with a high collar. Her dark hair was plaited around her head in a Grecian style. To the left of her, another woman in a floaty spotted dress was clutching a bunch of flowers and laughing straight at the camera. She had a different hairstyle, and looked quite a bit taller, but there was no mistaking that it was Ania.

'It's me at Mila's wedding. It was a gorgeous sunny day in the most wonderful July. She met her husband at teacher-training college and they were very happy. They had three children who all live in different parts of the world now. To answer your question, Julius, she did die, like we all will one day, but it was only a few years ago. Everybody was shocked that she managed to survive such a severe case of typhus and recover almost completely. She lived many, many happy years with her family near to where we grew up.'

'But what about before?' asked Julius. 'How did you survive the rest of the war, and what happened to Sommer?'

'Well, we stayed at the bakery for almost two years, which is why I like to think that I am an expert baker now. It was a safe place for us, because we were out of the way in the back rooms, and everyone trusted Roman. Even the soldiers seemed to leave him alone, maybe because a lot of their own provisions came from his ovens.

'Sommer came to see us every few weeks, always unannounced and always late at night. He was extremely moved by Mila's recovery and I'm sure that his visits brought him as much joy as they did us. During the time that we were there, he was promoted to the rank of commander. I could sense at first that he didn't want the new position, but he soon realised that there was one major advantage

– colleagues rarely questioned what he did. We never openly spoke about it, but I could tell that he helped other people in the same way that he helped Mila – I overheard him talking to Roman several times about contacts that he had across the city who might be able to take people in.

'Then, one day in early March of our second year at the bakery, he was moved to another part of the country. We hoped that we would hear from him, but we never did. The peculiar thing is that Mila always said to me that she felt as if he was there during all of the most important events in her life, and I felt exactly the same. I'm sure that he was secretly here, for example,' she said, tapping the wedding photo with her finger.

'Eventually, Roman got word that it was safe for us to travel back to our village and organised some transport for us through his friends. So, two and a half years after I set out on that train journey, I finally managed to make my way home. Through some miracle, my whole family managed to survive the war, although my father was missing for many months, and my mother and siblings had gone into hiding. Mila's mother was sadly never found. Mila was distraught, but I think, deep down, she may have expected it from the moment they got separated on the way to the ghetto. She came to live with us, which I thought was wonderful.'

I picked up the photo and traced the outline of the younger Ania's face with my finger, trying to get a few last moments with her before she disappeared. I felt strangely empty now that it was all over.

'Thank you, Ania,' I said. 'Thank you for telling us your story.'

'Thank *you*, for letting me share it. Do you know that I don't think I've told it to anyone like that – right from start to finish?' I could see that she too was sad it was over. 'Now you will not have another part to come back for, will you?'

She plaited her fingers in front of her on her lap and sighed. It was clear that she thought we wouldn't come to see her anymore and that made me incredibly sad.

'D'you want to tell your story to others?' Julius asked quietly. 'Because if you do, I think that there are heaps of people who would want to hear it.'

She looked up at us.

'We're doing the Second World War at school,' he explained. 'Miss Seymour would love it if somebody who had lived through it came to visit our class. Would you come?' he asked hopefully.

A flicker of a smile crossed over Ania's face.

'I'm not sure your class will want…'

'Of course they will!' I interrupted. 'Please, let me ask?'

'Well, you can ask. But I won't be offended if she says no, honestly. Telling you has been more than enough.'

TWENTY-TWO

Julius and I went to collect Ania from our school reception the following Friday afternoon. I could see that she had dressed up for the occasion especially. It also looked like it was a good-knee day, as the parrot was nowhere in sight.

'Gosh, I am nervous,' she said, fanning her face with a school brochure. 'I haven't spoken in front of such a large audience in years. I have a bad case of stage fright.'

'Don't be,' Julius told her. 'They'll all be gripped. Why don't you pretend that it's just Kat and me out there listening? You know that we think you're grand.'

And he was right, of course. Ania had to tell a much-shortened version of what Julius and I had heard, but everyone was engrossed. I could see that Gem was listening intently, despite telling Ruby and Dilly that I'd invited 'some boring old bag'.

I'd laughed when I overheard her saying that, and I realised I wasn't scared of her any more. It made me wonder why I'd allowed her to rule my life for so many years. She saw me laughing and scowled, but there was something in her look that made me certain that she was worried about what life at school would be like now so much had changed.

After what had happened in the hall, the rest of the class had begun to look at Gem differently too. It turned out that Arun had overheard her talking about how to get me and Julius back for what we'd done, and he'd worked out that she'd been behind the maggot incident and the dressing-up day affair. He decided to call off their date and Gem was gutted.

Julius and I had started spending much more time with Arun and his gang, who were all incredibly interesting. Jace was into comics, just like me, and he and another girl in our class, Hannah, decided to start up Comic Club every Tuesday lunchtime, where we'd read each other's strips and make suggestions of how to make them better.

'I think you'll agree,' said Miss Seymour at the end of the lesson, 'that history is best learned from the people who lived through it. A very inspirational account today from Mrs Jankowski.'

That afternoon, I walked out of school with Julius. The sky would soon be darkening, there was a gentle breeze in the air, and I linked my elbow through his as we walked over to Dad's car. I can't remember when I'd last felt so happy.

Dad dropped us off at Ania's and we sat round the table in the living room. Nowadays, Ania enjoyed looking through her living room window because Julius had done an amazing job tidying up the bushes and cutting the grass in the front garden – she could finally admire her beautiful dahlias and chrysanthemums.

Julius had brought round some celebratory cupcakes, and after we'd eaten these, Ania said, 'I have a surprise for you. Shut your eyes. OK, now come forward a couple of steps. Perfect. Now you can open them.'

I gasped when I saw it. In the middle of the main wall of the conservatory, was the breath-taking portrait of Mila in full colour. Her plait was a deep, beautiful brown, each strand defined with a tiny brushstroke. Her cheeks were different shades of blush, her freckles carefully painted in tiny, honey-coloured specks. But the most awesome thing about the painting was her eyes, which were so many wonderful hues of sky, ocean and sapphire – they danced in the beams of sunshine that came through the garden windows and I could see how much they made Ania smile.

Her portrait was next to Sommer's – the way that Ania had positioned them, it seemed as if he was looking over at her protectively, making sure that she came to no harm.

'You helped me bring her to life,' she said. 'I started working on her again as soon as I began to tell you our story, but I didn't want you to see this before it was finished. You know now that my secret search for Mila finally paid off. There were so many times when I doubted that it would. But I suppose it wasn't just a search for her. It was a search for kindness, for a little beam of light in the darkness.'

'They're wonderful,' I told her, as I gazed at the portraits. 'They are absolutely wonderful.'

'Don't forget that you still owe me something,' she said to me.

'What's that?'

'*Girl 38*. You promised me the finished edition, as soon as I'd told you my whole story.'

I grinned. 'You'll have it tomorrow,' I told her. There was a final scene that I had to finish. I hadn't had the time to put it in the copy I'd given to Gem, but I felt it was very important to include.

The Vilks helped Girl 38 to carry the food back to her shipmates, who were all in awe of her. As they sat around the half-fixed spaceship, eating the juiciest berries, they wondered how such a small person had managed to overpower an army of giant wolves. Many of them thought that she must have sent a deadly arrow right into the heart of the Vilk King, which had made the rest of the pack fear her.

But only Girl 38 knew the truth. She'd seen it when she'd first looked into the Vilk's eyes. There was more light in them than darkness, and that was all that mattered.

She cut the largest of the apples that she could find and offered half to her new friend. They ate together as they watched the brilliant electric blue sunset disappear behind the horizon of Planet U.

ACKNOWLEDGEMENTS

Firstly a big thank you to my grandmother, whose experiences as a teenager during the Second World War formed the inspiration for Ania's story. As a family, we long ago realised that nothing we do quite matches up to jumping from a moving train.

Thank you to Kate, my wonderful agent, for believing in this story from the start and persuading me to tell it.

Thank you to my patient and encouraging editor Fiona, to Lauren and the rest of the amazing team at Head of Zeus for all their hard work in getting *Girl 38* into the best possible shape.

Thank you to all my family and friends who believed I had a second book in me and supported me in writing it whilst having two demanding little ladies at home. I am hugely grateful.

Ewa Jozefkowicz,
London, November 2018